...ions can't have any fun
...for power, trained for might
...boxer can't escape the fight
...ry racehorse needs a goat
...drowning man must love the boat
...fall to your knees and kiss the feet
That saved you from becoming meat.

From the private collection of Jesper Idyll.

RaWaR

What's The Stigmata?
Kakophony Records, 2020

1. Pieta
Pieta means pity, and what you did was shitty
We just want to be ourselves, dark and strange an...
...ill you hit us with your stones
...a boring plastic little drones
...we will come back from the dead
...live forever in your head
...a, Shangri-La, the unpure can't know Nirvan...
...ne us, shoot us, crucify us
...not confuse cruel with pious

Caterpillar of Salt
...spiration, transformation
...ead to body and water to wine
...tay the same and die inside
...ke the knife and draw the line

Alter Altar
...rated, hexed, fated
...ome to me soft, sweet, sedated
...lay you on the stone
...waiting, cold as bone
...to me of your free will
...ur heart, be silent, still
...rself up to my whims
...rself to me, to him
...you scream and cry
...y until you die

...vet kisses
...reak and maim you
...rk you from within, make you one with hi...
...hen a good lay becomes prey the border dim...

...Jonathan Livingston Steven Seag...
...There's no such thing as never
Only now, only forever
...ere's no such thing as sin
...mistakes you commit, again and again
...show me who you are
...neat bag driven by the stuff of stars
...ly cowards run
...e edge of the cliff is the starting gun, oh yeah

...e Die Diana
...d me your secrets
...ll me no lies
...ake of your heart
...The ultimate prize
...Wash yourself clean
...Whiter than snow
...I am the stag, you are the doe

Dark Angel (Unreleased)
You are magic, tragic, the one I need
You are my blood, the air I breathe
You see the truth amidst the lies
A glittering moth among butterflies
Every artist needs a seed
You're in mylungs, the air I breathe
Angeline, Angeline,
Prettiest angel I've ever seen

From the personal collection of Jesper Idyll.

...ings Got Dark
...ophony Records, 2022

Gone Too Soon
...too soon, you're gone too soon
...sun is slaughtered by the moon
...autumn follows summer's swoon
...re gone too soon, gone too soon
...ved you then, I know you...

What's
Kakophony...

1. Pieta
Pieta mean...
We just wa...
Still you k...

"With a punk attitude and a gothic soul, Delilah S. Dawson's *House of Idyll* delves into the cost of making great art — what it gives and takes. There's a fine line between opportunity and darkness — will you walk it? Remember: only cowards run."

ANGELA 'A.G.' SLATTER, award-winning author of *The Crimson Road*

"This was a trip and a half — part rock anthem, part isolation horror, and totally intoxicating. Delilah S. Dawson delivers this story with a guitar in one hand and a knife in the other. A seductive exploration of art, fame, and the desire to be seen that is every bit as consuming as an 80s power ballad — and twice as difficult to get out of your head."

JOSH WINNING, author of *Heads Will Roll*

HOUSE
OF IDYLL

Also by Delilah S. Dawson

It Will Only Hurt for a Moment
Bloom
The Violence
Guillotine

THE BLUD SERIES
Wicked as They Come
Wicked as She Wants
Wicked After Midnight
Wicked Ever After

THE HIT SERIES
Hit
Strike

Servants of the Storm
Midnight at the Houdini

Mine
Camp Scare

Star Wars: Phasma
Star Wars Galaxy's Edge: Black Spire
Star Wars Inquisitor: Rise of the Red Blade
Disney Mirrorverse: Pure of Heart
The Minecraft Mob Squad Series
Dungeons & Dragons: Ravenloft: Heir of Strahd

THE SHADOW SERIES,
WRITTEN AS LILA BOWEN
Wake of Vultures
Conspiracy of Ravens
Malice of Crows
Treason of Hawks

HOUSE OF IDYLL

DELILAH S.
DAWSON

TITAN BOOKS

House of Idyll
Hardback edition ISBN: 9781835414217
Hardback signed edition ISBN: 9781835416815
E-book edition ISBN: 9781835414224

Published by Titan Books
A division of Titan Publishing Group Ltd
144 Southwark Street, London SE1 0UP
www.titanbooks.com

First edition: September 2025
10 9 8 7 6 5 4 3 2 1

A CIP catalogue record for this title is available from the British Library.

EU RP (for authorities only)
eucomply OÜ, Pärnu mnt. 139b-14, 11317 Tallinn, Estonia
hello@eucompliancepartner.com, +3375690241

Set in Agmena Pro by Richard Mason.

Printed and bound by CPI Group (UK) Ltd, Croydon CR0 4YY.

For those about to rock:
We salute you.

You can't run and you can't hide
Did you almost live or have you almost died
They told you to blend in with the herd
But conformity is a dirty word
You're a unicorn, you're a unicorn
From your blade-edged hooves to your stabbing horn
Be tall and proud
Get big, get loud
Be their number one, not tragedy porn

"UNICORN," TRACK #1 ON BLACK IDYLL,
(RE)HEARSE, KAKOPHONY RECORDS, 2014.

BEFORE

INTERVIEWER:

BLACK IDYLL IS THE TOP-SELLING BAND IN
THE WORLD, FINISHING YOUR FIRST SOLD-OUT
INTERNATIONAL STADIUM TOUR, TOPPING ALL THE
CHARTS WITH YOUR FIRST ALBUM. HOW DOES IT
FEEL?

JESPER IDYLL:

(LAUGHS) SO BIG I CAN'T WRAP MY ARMS AROUND
IT. INCONCEIVABLE. SHAPELESS. EXPLOSIVE.
A FORCE BEYOND UNDERSTANDING. HEAVY. LIKE
GRAVITY. IT'S A GREAT GIFT, BUT IT'S OUT
OF MY HANDS. ALL I CAN CONTROL IS THE ART.
THE MUSIC.

INTERVIEWER:

SO HOW IS THE BAND GETTING ALONG WITHOUT
VIVIAN? THE FIVE OF YOU CAME UP TOGETHER,
AND IT SEEMS LIKE A TRAGEDY THAT SHE NEVER
GOT TO SEE YOUR ALBUM GO PLATINUM.

JESPER IDYLL:

VIVIAN WAS THE HEART OF BLACK IDYLL. THE
SUN AROUND WHICH WE ALL ORBITED. WE MISS
HER EVERY DAY. WE WOULDN'T BE HERE WITHOUT
HER—WITHOUT HER VOICE, HER WORDS, HER BLOOD,
SWEAT, AND TEARS. WE OWE HER EVERYTHING.

INTERVIEWER:

THE WAY SHE DIED—

JESPER IDYLL:

THIS INTERVIEW IS OVER.

Welcome to the worst day of
  your life
It's time to face the bloodied
  butcher's knife
The razor's edge between then
  and now
Are you the abattoir or the
  suckling cow?

"FACE THE KNIFE," TRACK #2 ON BLACK IDYLL,
(RE)HEARSE, KAKOPHONY RECORDS, 2014.

1

Sometimes a moment is filled with infinite possibility: a letter opened but unread, a phone ringing but unanswered, a morning that has only just begun and is thus far splendid even though it will surely be ruined once the front door is unlocked and the customers begin to arrive. Three percolators are merrily chirping as they turn oily beans into wake-up juice, and not a single splatter of cream mars the counter. Silver pitchers sit, shiny and clean, waiting to steam milk for people who think that an extra dry cappuccino is actually good. The fridge is stocked, the rags are bleached, and the floor smells like lemons. The sun is shining—because the sun is always shining in LA. Anything could happen today.

That's what Angelina Yves tells herself.

Anything could happen.

What will most likely happen is that she will get shouted at for not knowing a secret recipe that doesn't exist, and she will burn a finger pouring a boiling hot drink into a Stanley cup for a woman with a hypoallergenic dog in her purse, and she will take home far fewer tips than she deserves because she's pretty sure that Greyson is stealing from the tip jar. It's such a cliché, the wannabe singer-songwriter working as a barista at a Hollywood café, scribbling lyrics on napkins during her timed break, praying one of her raw-voiced original songs goes viral online, but she needs the health insurance and at least they pay over minimum wage.

As it turns out, and much to her annoyance, her dad was right: the only job for people with music degrees is teaching other people how to get music degrees. If her favorite professor's eccentric aunt didn't have an extra room and need a part-time caretaker, there's no way Angelina could afford to live anywhere near LA, and yet here she is, working so hard to make her dreams come true that she doesn't really dream at night anymore.

"Zosia?" she calls, hoping she's reading the name right: Zoe-see-a.

A red-taloned hand swipes the cup. "It's pronounced Sasha." No tip there.

"No actress can go by Emily or Kate anymore. They've gotta stand out. I had a Kaylee yesterday who'd added two Hs and half a dozen vowels," Lauren says, leaning in to where Angelina is now hiding behind the espresso machine. "Kuh-hay-uh-huh-luh-hee." She sounds like she's panting. "Almost ran out of breath trying to call her name. Don't let it get to you." Lauren is in her fifties and was once a C-level actor, back in the eighties when perfection couldn't be forced with surgery. These days, she's an unflappable battle-ax, and she's the closest thing Angelina has to a friend in this city. "Didn't you close last night?"

Angelina rubs her eyes, careful not to smudge her heavily smoky eye. "Yep. Rick texted me after midnight asking me to open because Greyson had to study."

"Can't let his nephew get sleepy now, can we? Jeez. Nepotism and Hollywood." Lauren shakes her bleached curls, still teased to the heavens. "You'd think it only happened in the movies, but it's everywhere."

And yes, it's true, but Angelina still believes that hard work and a good attitude have value. If she stopped believing that, she'd fall apart. She'd stop writing songs. She'd give up.

She makes the next drink, trying to inject it with what little artistry the job allows. This shop is so busy that there is no time for friendly chitchat with the customers, no time to draw swans in the foam. She is a machine, her only goal to avoid being yelled at. Everyone is in a hurry, everyone is angry, and it is always, always her fault.

"Beavis?" she calls, knowing the teen boys will snicker before the tall one swipes his drink, but grateful that it didn't say Saoirse or Björn. She knows how to pronounce Beavis. The next drink, at least, is simple: a green tea for Sol. She double cups it so he won't burn himself and, yes, come back to yell at her.

"Sol?"

She holds out the cup, and the guy who takes it is so beautiful that it's kind of disturbing—and yet he's also vaguely familiar. They lock eyes for a moment, and he smiles and blinks once, like an owl. He's wearing all white, his dark skin making the contrast all the more striking. White slim-fit jeans, white loafers, white linen shirt, a silver necklace nestled in the unbuttoned V, and long, black locs loosely bound. He looks like a movie star, but if he was, she would definitely recognize him.

"Thank you, love," he tells her with a posh British accent, and he sounds like he means it. He slides a twenty toward her and winks.

"Thank you. Have a good day," she tells him. Her eyes flash to the camera in the corner, and as soon as he's gone, she goes to deposit the twenty in the tip jar. There's writing on it, and she looks more closely before abandoning it among the ones and spare change.

Oddly, the bill is stamped with a lyric from a popular song she loved when she was in high school.

> *There's no such thing as never*
> *Only now, only forever.*

It's a little trite, but it brings back fond memories of when she was a teenager, sitting in her closet, hiding from her parents, singing along to Black Idyll the summer they hit it big. She begged to go to the concert, but it was a firm no. Her dad was nearing sixty then and her mom has always been as boring and limp as a wet lasagna noodle, and they both refused to acknowledge any music that wasn't glorifying God or

America. For a time, Black Idyll was her whole world, and she was half in love with Jesper Idyll. Everyone was. Both because he played teen heartthrob Carter Dunaway on *This Is How It Is* and because he was the lead singer for a band of beautiful teen boys in all black who seemed to channel all the rage, weirdness, and yearning of the collective generation. What a strange thing to find on a crisp twenty that will become possibly two crumpled ones in Angelina's pocket when they divvy up the tip jar later on.

Angelina has forgotten about the handsome man and his lovely but ultimately useless tip when her phone rings an hour later. The number is unfamiliar, but the caller ID says it's from her college. She's not supposed to take calls at work, but...

"Hello?"

"Angelina, it's Doctor Bradley."

Despite the heat of the milk steamer and the sweaty hairs straggling against her temples Angelina's blood goes cold. Usually, Dr. Bradley is just Lisa, and usually, Lisa calls on her own cell phone to dish about office politics and complain about how no TA will ever compare to her favorite student and future Grammy-award winner.

"Hi, Li— Dr. Bradley. What's up?"

A sigh. "Look, I'm sorry about this, but Aunt Barb says it's not working out. She says you steal from her."

Angelina gasps. "You know she has dementia, and I think you know me well enough to know that I would never steal from anyone."

"I know all that. And it's stupid—she said you stole a

ceramic turtle from her collection. Which— why? Nobody wants that shit. But she's not going to let this go. I think we're just going to have to call a service."

Angelina's mind is racing, trying to find some way to stay exactly where she is, to not lose what she has. "I'll get her a new ceramic turtle. Ten more. I'll buy cameras and install them. Please, Lisa. You know what this means to me."

Everything. It means everything.

This is the only way she can afford to be here. Even with free rent, even working two jobs, she can barely afford it.

And if she's not here...

Her dream is over.

The only way to get jobs in LA is to be in LA. She can't busk on the streets of Ellijay, Georgia and hope to get discovered.

And if she has to go home...

No.

She can't.

Not after how she ended things with her parents.

"She called the cops, kiddo. Told 'em you're a thief. And also, oddly enough, a robot. So they called me. She needs to be under actual medical supervision. Dementia plus Capgras syndrome? It's only going to get worse."

No wonder the old lady had been giving her the side-eye. Angelina had thought they were getting along just fine, had done everything in her power to be the perfect roommate/ nurse. And yet. And yet.

"So... so maybe I stay with her but don't help her out? She won't even see me. She doesn't leave her room."

"Kiddo, once she thinks you're a robot who steals turtles, you can't un-ring that bell. We can give you two weeks to find a new situation. I'm sorry. You're talented and you deserve better, and I know you were doing a good job, but it just isn't going to work out."

"I wiped her ass!" Angelina barks. "I have cleaned up her pee puddles, and I have remade her Cream of Wheat three times every morning until it's perfectly smooth, and we both know I'm neither a robot nor a thief!" Her voice is rising, and Rick is walking toward her, with his stupid pleated khakis and tucked in Hawaiian shirt that make him look like a tropical snowman.

"I know, and I'm sorry—"

The milk she's been steaming boils over the sides of the silver pitcher, burning her hand. She drops the piping hot metal and screams, "Fuck a duck!" The pitcher lands on her foot, and scalding milk soaks her ankle and splatters across the floor mats as the steamer continues to spurt steam into her face.

"Outside. Now!" Rick grinds out through clenched teeth.

Angelina feels the tears rising and tries to blink them back down. "I'm sorry—"

"Was that for my upside-down caramel ribbon crunch macchiato with extra whip and seven sugars?" asks a bored teen girl with extensions to her butt who's holding a thirty-thousand-dollar handbag. "Because I'm in, like, a hurry." She holds up the latest iPhone, shoving it in Angelina's face to record whatever bad behavior follows.

Angelina looks down at the cracked old phone in her own

hand, then at her guitar-callused fingers now boiled red and curled up like a dead bug, coated in tan milk froth.

"Kid, you there?" Lisa's voice in her phone is so far away.

Everything is.

"My drink?" the girl asks again. "Because if I have to wait one more second, I want a refund. Do you even know how many followers I have?" She turns around, her back to Angelina so she can film them both in selfie mode. "Fam, I just had *the worst* experience with this ho. It's boycott time. Make this bitch go viral. Do not ever go to—"

Angelina looks directly into the girl's brand new iPhone and starts to sing the chorus of Lily Allen's "Fuck You" while she strips off her apron for the last time.

Have you ever felt so alone that you
    wanted to die?
Have you ever felt so alone that you
    wanted to cry?
(But pretty boys don't cry)
Have you ever felt like just a tiny
    pinprick in the sky?
(See the comets passing by)
So far away from the Earth you know
Yet you're stuck on cursed ground with
    no wings to fly.

"PRETTY BOYS DON'T CRY," TRACK #3 ON BLACK IDYLL,
NEVER RHYME FRIEND WITH END, KAKOPHONY RECORDS, 2016.

2

Angelina has just been fired for the first—

Ha!

No, the second time.

First by Dr. Bradley five minutes ago, and now by Rick the Tropical Snowman for "conduct unbecoming in the workplace". Never mind that Greyson sometimes writes "Nice tits!" on the cups of attractive teen girls when he actually bothers to show up. No, apparently cursing as a contralto while sustaining third-degree burns on some wannabe influencer's TikTok channel is enough to end her coffee career.

She sits on the bench two stores down, her tote bag slumped beside her. Her hand is crumpled like a boiled rabbit in her lap as tears stream down her face. She should've grabbed a wad of napkins on the way out, but Rick got pretty pushy, especially when she refused to stop singing. She didn't really want to be a barista, anyway. She wants to be a singer—she *is* a singer—and now she is also homeless and jobless, all in one fell swoop. She used to think the starving artist was such a romantic motif, and then she learned that it's hard to write good material without electricity and a comfortable chair.

So she does the first thing that comes to mind: She puts her hat out on the concrete and starts singing. As much as she would prefer to perform originals, she knows full well that the best tips come from songs that feel familiar and evoke emotions. Today, feeling what she feels, that means Bon Jovi's "Blaze of Glory." She's three songs in with ten dollars and some change when a car rolls up to the curb, one of those huge black SUVs that rich people take to the airport. The back-seat window rolls down, and a familiar face appears. It's Sol, he of the green tea and twenty-dollar tip. His amber eyes are filled with concern, his long fingers with white-painted nails tapping along the edge of the sunglass-black window as he listens.

She holds the last note, daring him to interrupt, and when she's done, he asks, "The worst day of your life?" with a curious mix of empathy and bemusement.

"Third worst," she corrects. "So far." She sniffles, willing herself to meet his gaze without shame. He raises an eyebrow, and it feels like a dare, so she continues. "When I was nine, I tried to peek in my grandmother's coffin at her funeral, the lid fell and broke my finger, and I toppled on the ground, hit my head, and peed myself. And then there was homecoming, but I don't tell strangers that story."

She is aware that the tears are still streaming down her face.

She doesn't care.

What does she have to lose now that she's lost everything?

"You're an intriguing woman with a hell of a voice."

A tear traces down her cheek, past her lips, and falls off her chin.

"Intriguing doesn't pay the bills, sadly, and as of today, music doesn't either."

"You're pretty when you cry, you know. You could model."

She snorts. "Yeah, no thanks. That's what the kids these days call a red flag."

She picks up her hat and shoulders her bag, and he says, "Wait."

They're eye to eye now. Soft music fumbles from the car along with cool air and... is that the scent of jasmine?

Sol seems to be considering something.

"So what will you do?" he asks.

Simple enough words, but she recognizes the familiar cadence. The song has been stuck in her head since she read the lyrics stamped on his twenty. This guy must be a Black Idyll hardcore fan, for all that he looks like a Prada model.

"'Show me what's real, which face is true,'" she sings softly so only he can hear it.

He smiles. "Go on."

So she keeps singing lyrics she knows by heart. "'Only cowards run. The edge of the cliff is the starting gun.'" She mimics the finger-gun pistol shot Jesper Idyll used every time he performed that line in his all-black Goth Mr. Darcy tailcoat and fluttery blouse. "Are you saying I'm at the edge and getting fired is my starting gun?" A mad half-laugh, half-hiccup escapes her. "God, Black Idyll. Whatever happened to those guys?"

The car door swings open, and Sol settles back into the darkness of the SUV.

"Come and see," he says from the shadows.

Angelina is caught between laughter and curiosity.

What's happening now is absurd.

Either she's having the worst luck on the planet or the best.

No job, no home... and this beautiful man is either scouting her as a model or taking her somewhere quiet to put her head in a jar and make scones out of her rib bacon while he sings Black Idyll songs wearing a bathrobe made of her skin.

"What is this?" she asks.

"An invitation."

"To what?"

Sol chuckles from the darkness. "That's the thing about the cliff's edge, love. Either you jump or you run. You don't get to find out what's on the other side if you don't jump."

Is he... admitting he's going to murder her?

She turns on her phone and shares her location with Lauren, Lisa, and her mom. Then she walks around to the back of the car, takes a picture of the license plate, and sends that to all three of them.

Getting in this car. If you don't hear from me again, track my location and tell the police, she texts.

Now that she's made a point of capturing the tags, she's surprised the car hasn't streaked away—as far as a car can streak in LA traffic. It's still idling.

"This is a perfectly safe situation, you know," Sol says. "But I can appreciate your caution. If you're comfortable with your safeguards, you have ten seconds to get in, and then the cliff disappears."

Angelina looks down at her hat. She looks back at the café. She thinks about how it will feel, going home to Crazy Barb Who Thinks She's a Robotic Thief and frantically looking for an affordable place to stay in a place where nowhere is affordable. What has she got to lose?

She steps up into the vehicle.

There's no such thing as never
Only now, only forever
There's no such thing as sin
Just mistakes you commit, again
 and again
So show me who you are
A meat bag driven by the stuff
 of stars
Only cowards run
The edge of the cliff is the
 starting gun, oh yeah

"JONATHAN LIVINGSTON STEVEN SEAGAL," TRACK #5
ON BLACK IDYLL, RaWaR, KAKOPHONY RECORDS, 2018.

3

"So, for real, what is this?"

Sol doesn't answer. He's in the other bucket seat, one long foot splayed over his knee as he taps into his sleek white phone. He looks like he has never been more relaxed in his life, like he couldn't find the word stressed in the dictionary if offered six figures. Angelina, on the other hand, is on full alert. She's expecting a bag over her head, a gun in her ribs, a chilled bottled water with a hypodermic hole hidden under the wrapper. There is no divider between the front and back seats, at least, no signs that the car has been customized to hold prisoners. The driver is an older white man in a black suit who looks unnervingly like her father.

"Sir, am I being abducted?" Angelina calls to him.

The man looks back at her in the rearview mirror, eyes crinkled up like a mall Santa. "No, honey. He's on the up and up. Like he said, perfectly safe. I don't go abducting no girls."

He's got a New York accent—and looks like he's busted his knuckles multiple times.

"Where are we going?"

At that, Sol looks up at her. He has an ethereal beauty, with cheekbones that could cut glass. But there's something puckish about him, something impish and delighted and pleased. Something weirdly, glaringly authentic.

This is not a trait she sees very often in LA. Or anywhere.

"You mentioned modeling. Am I... being scouted?" she asks.

She knows she's pretty, with her milky white skin, dark tumbling hair, and haunted gray eyes. And she knows she's lost weight since arriving in California and being forced to count every penny against her pride. She's not tall enough to model, but... well, there was a girl under five feet on *America's Next Top Model* once, so at five-seven, it's not impossible.

His full lips twitch with a smile as he looks out the window. "Something like that."

The driver navigates out of the city and onto a highway. After Angelina's thousandth question, Sol shakes a finger at her. "All will be revealed in time. Just enjoy the ride."

Enjoy... the ride? Through LA? Not likely. It's either traffic or oil derricks or charred earth or new construction. Angelina scrolls through her phone looking for a living situation and then a job, but these are the same ads she's seen again and again, and she's fairly certain they're all scams. She hasn't gotten a single nibble for anything besides the barista gig, and she's applied to something full time every day. Her bachelor's in music isn't worth the paper it's printed on, much less the loans she'll be paying off until she's fifty.

You OK? Lauren texts.

So far. But watch my location in case I disappear.

Nothing from Lisa, nothing from her mother, who generally leaves her phone in her purse and only uses it to scroll through Facebook joke groups when she's in a doctor's waiting room.

As for Sol, he regards his phone with a preternatural calm. They drive so far into the forest that Angelina's worry kicks up another notch, but no one has attempted to take her phone away. She still has bars. Her location is still sharing. She is terrified but also curious. She has never been gently kidnapped by a beautiful person before.

It's been an hour and a half, and she's on the edge of asking about stopping to use the restroom when they turn down a recently paved road marked by two white stone pillars. They come to a guardhouse crafted of the same stone, and a man in all white waves them through a grand set of white iron gates.

Now they're on a long drive bordered by heavy bushes and tall trees that kiss overhead. After a while, the trees open up to show a house —

No. A mansion.

A compound, really.

One huge white villa flanked by numerous smaller cabins and a two-story barn. The forest curves around with the impossible perfection of a Hollywood movie backdrop, holding the snow-white buildings in a cozy sort of hug. It's early afternoon, and the deep blue sky arches overhead, containing the sprawling valley like a snow globe that has captured one bright and perfect moment.

Yes, if Sol is part of this place, he is probably on the up and up.

Whoever owns this compound—or even has enough money to rent it for one night—can buy anything they want, including, most likely, human beings. They wouldn't need to snatch pretty girls off the street. Angelina isn't sure if this makes her feel more comfortable... or less.

The SUV follows the drive around to the massive home's front steps and stops. The driver opens the door for Sol, and he gets out and offers Angelina his hand.

"I can get out of a car," she mutters as she scrambles to her feet, wishing she weren't quite so covered in coffee stains.

"Courtesy is not a command," he tells her as if reciting a beloved poem. "But a gift."

He walks in the villa's open door, and she follows. The car drives away. It feels as if she is in another world, spirited away to Faerie. They are in a round foyer with a floor of polished white stone. A unicorn made of white-stained driftwood dominates the space, half guard dog and half welcoming committee. Everything is white and gold and beautiful. The air is perfumed with white flowers and sandalwood, white fans twirling lazily on white ceilings. The windows are thrown open as if inviting the world to French kiss the home's every eager mouth. There is a feeling of care here, of choice, of craftsmanship. Not a single corner has been cut. In a world of gray, this place has been rinsed clean, its beautiful ivory bones bravely exposed.

Sol takes the curving stairwell of wood blocks up to the second floor. Angelina has decided that she will follow him until he tells her to stop because she has to know what's going on here, what this place is and why she's been invited. She will go as far as they let her go, whoever they are. She has never witnessed such wealth in her life, and she would happily sleep on the floor under the spread hooves of the murderous wood unicorn if it meant that she could stay a while longer.

The floors upstairs are honey gold wood, their waxy shine making her wish she was barefoot instead of wearing squeaky, coffee-soaked Converse high tops. It feels like desecration to be dressed in ratty jeans and a plain black shirt here. Sol's all-white ensemble fits in as naturally as a sheep among its flock. He leads her down a long hallway and knocks on the heavy wooden door at the end.

"Enter, friend," calls a man's voice.

Sol stands back, inclines his head toward the door.

"You're not coming, too?" Angelina asks, suddenly shy.

"Welcome to the cliff. If you take the first step, you have to take it on your own." He winks and heads back down the hall, leaving her alone with the door.

Angelina wishes for a mirror, a clean outfit, a hairbrush. She knows her eyeliner and mascara have forged graffiti down her cheeks, knows her long hair is tangled from the way she shoved her hands in it when she sat outside on that bench, pondering her fate and twisting locks angrily into curls.

She also knows that the person on the other side of the door must know her situation and still want to see her, so... well, they get what they get. She's the same person whether she's in a prom gown or her dingiest pajamas. She twists the knob and pushes open the door.

This room, like the rest of the villa, is all the same uniform, milky, pure, unmarred white. French doors open up to a balcony, filmy white curtains whispering playfully with the breeze. She half-expected to find a massive master bedroom, a four-poster bed and sticky casting couch, but instead, there is a profound and airy emptiness broken up only by two round cushions in the middle of a circular white wool rug. On one of these cushions, dressed in a white tunic and white linen pants, barefoot and cross-legged and staring at her with his trademark pale blue eyes, sits Jesper Idyll, singer of Black Idyll and celebrity crush of her youth and still the most beautiful man she's ever seen.

"Tell me, Angelina," he says in a voice she knows as well as her own heartbeat. "What is the source of all beauty?"

Pieta means pity, and what you did was shitty
We just want to be ourselves, dark and strange and pretty
Still you hit us with your stones
You boring plastic little drones
But we will come back from the dead
To live forever in your head
Pieta, Shangri-La, the unpure can't know Nirvana
Stone us, shoot us, crucify us
Do not confuse cruel with pious

"PIETA," TRACK #1 ON BLACK IDYLL, WHAT'S THE
STIGMATA?, KAKOPHONY RECORDS, 2020.

4

Angelina wants to ask if she's being punked, if someone is recording this, but she also wants to fall into the limpid pools of Jesper's eyes and die happily in his arms like the girl in the video for "Pieta." Not one of her all-time favorite songs, but that video was the twenty-first century version of Madonna's "Like a Prayer." In it, Jesper was dressed as a crucified Jesus, complete with a beaded loincloth designed by Donatella Versace and a jagged, bloody hole near his six-pack, and the dead girl he lovingly held had been bullied to death at school for dressing emo. It didn't hurt that Jesper looked a lot like White Jesus, with his piercing, pool-blue eyes and long, flowing blond hair.

The conservatives tried to cancel him, and that's when Black Idyll went from megastars to legends. Their drummer, Nico, got grazed by a bullet from an angry Baptist with a sniper rifle but he just put on a helmet and a bulletproof vest for the next show and kept playing. Just like the song said, the death threats only helped them to rise.

So yes, this is unmistakably Jesper Idyll.

The Jesper Idyll.

And he has just asked Angelina a question.

What is the source of all beauty?

It's a pretty strange conversation opener, but from what she knows of Jesper, he's a pretty strange guy. He writes and sings all the Black Idyll songs while also playing guitar and sometimes piano and, for one song, bagpipes. Their earliest albums were all about being angry, alone, an outcast, misunderstood, how the world was against the weirdos. As the years went on, they sang about rebellion, pushing boundaries, fighting for what you love, never giving up or becoming complacent, sacrificing everything for art. Their last album was more experimental, with one song that included singing bowls and the clicking of sperm whales and another featuring collabs with Skrillex and Childish Gambino. They haven't toured in two years; they haven't had to. With nearly a decade of platinum albums, sold-out shows, and Jesper's movie career, plus Manny's clever financial investments, Jesper is on the billionaire's index and the rest of the band is set up for life.

No wonder this place is so sprawling, so luxurious, so beautiful.

If it belongs to Black Idyll—to Jesper Idyll—what else would it be?

He is waiting for her, staring at her with an intensity she has never before experienced. This must be what it feels like to lock eyes with a leopard in the midst of dense jungle foliage, pores open and blood screaming, heart pounding in your ears. She feels unbalanced, standing while he sits, but she has not been invited to sit, and the cushion doesn't look particularly comfortable.

He says nothing. He is patient. He is as still as a statue.

"What is the source of all beauty?" she repeats like a spelling bee champion.

He nods once, slowly.

This is important.

As Sol said, the cliff's edge.

She's a songwriter, goddammit. She lives for poetry.

So all she has to do is put words in the right order to create the perfect answer that will impress Jesper Idyll, who has won five Grammys and an Oscar.

Is this... related to the lyrics of a Black Idyll song?

No.

She would've recognized anything like that immediately.

She has to do this on her own, using what she knows of this reclusive polymath genius.

"Nature or the knife," she finally says. "Randomly given or purposefully stolen."

And Jesper's face changes, a marble angel come to life.

Those sensuous lips turn up into a genuine smile, those endless blue eyes sparkle. He stands gracefully, almost like he's weightless, and steps forward to take her hands. He's taller than her, and although she would've expected his hands to be the smooth accessories of a pampered prince, instead she feels the hard-won callouses on every finger, just like her own.

"What's the most beautiful thing you've ever seen?"

"A homeless man offering water to a bumblebee during a heat wave," she says without thinking. It haunts her to this day, how the old man's burnished wrinkles quirked up around his toothless lips in delight as he watched the tiny insect sip water from the cap of his only water bottle.

"What's the ugliest thing?"

"The fussy way my rapist buckled his belt when he was done."

Jesper's eyes briefly fill with sorrow. He blinks, and it retreats like a wave on the sand.

"What do you want most in the world, Angelina?"

It's as if he's ensorcelled her somehow. She's been lost in his eyes since he took her hands, unable to avert her gaze. There is no room, no villa, no compound, no forest, no world beyond this white space. There is only her and this other being, soul to soul, and she answers his questions as if he's pulling them directly from her heart.

"The freedom to make music without worrying about how to stay alive. I want to write and sing."

"And?"

It's like he can tell she's holding her tongue, that she doesn't want to admit the second part.

"And I want to be wildly successful and prove my parents wrong and hear thunderous applause. For me."

He nods eagerly, like he's proud of her—

No, like he's encouraging her.

Like this is exactly what he wanted to hear.

Her hands are still in his, and she's holding them so, so still, desperate not to break this spell, like he's a butterfly that's alighted on her skin and she would die before scaring him away with a single twitch.

"What if you could have all that and more?" he asks.

Even his voice is musical.

Deep but soft, masculine but gentle, powerful but sweet.

This isn't an iron fist in a velvet glove; it's molten chocolate dripping down a knife.

Something about him draws the words out of her, the sun calling forth the seed.

She used to fall asleep to this voice.

She has heard him in her dreams.

"What if I could have everything? Then I would welcome it with open arms," she says, unsure what he means but very interested in...

Jesus, anything.

Anything he will offer her, she will take it.

A job, an internship.

Hell, she'll put on a sequined leotard and be a backup dancer if it means she doesn't have to move back home.

"Angelina, do you believe in beauty?"

"Of course."

"And do you believe that art is the pursuit of beauty?"

That... gives her pause.

She doesn't want to disagree with him, but she is also not willing to lie.

If she did, she's fairly certain he would know, somehow.

"Sometimes art is ugly," she says haltingly, feeling her way in the dark to the answer she knows is true. "Because the world is often ugly, and art can be a spotlight. It exposes what's there, forces it to the surface, makes people look at what they'd rather not see. But even in that ugliness, there is beauty."

Much to her surprise, Jesper bursts out laughing. "Oh, fuck. That's a good answer." He squeezes her hands and releases her. "Solomon?"

Sol — *Solomon* — appears in the doorway.

"Give her a tour, would you?"

In the time it took Angelina to look at Solomon, Jesper has sunk back onto his cushion. He sits in lotus position, hands open like flowers where they rest on his knees. His eyes are closed, his long eyelashes casting shadows on his sculpted cheeks. He was here, but now he is somewhere else, unreachable.

"Angelina?" Solomon calls from the door.

Feeling like she's just met the Wizard of Oz and has been summarily dismissed, she follows Solomon back down the hall and stairs. He does not speak until they're on the front porch.

"So you passed the first test," he says. "Now I'll show you what we're doing here, and you can decide if you want to be a part of our little experiment."

Softly the world coalesces around her, her senses coming back online as he leads her along a dirt path. Birdsong, the rush of wind in the trees, gentle voices, the scent of incense burning nearby. A flash of white catches Angelina's eye, and she sees two willowy women walking in long white skirts and white tank tops, their Botticelli hair billowing behind them. They carry woven baskets full of freshly pulled vegetables, rich dirt still clinging to the carrots.

"Is this... a cult?" Angelina asks.

Solomon bursts out laughing. "A cult? No. Closer to a very wealthy commune, maybe. Look, Jesper is a billionaire. He has more money than he could ever spend in a hundred lives no matter how many gold toilets and yachts and Bugattis he wanted—which is none. So he found this ranch and decided to turn it into an incubator. Artists can stay here for free and finally have the time and space to create. We sponsor galleries, exhibitions, events, charities, scientific breakthroughs. We act as angel investors in businesses that will keep the world livable and beautiful. We make movies and produce new bands and boost new designers. Everything we do is formally registered with the state. We have 501c-3 status. There is no religious aspect, you don't have to give up anything. And we're not going to take your phone or try to cut you off from the outside world."

They're passing by a row of— well, at first she thought they were cabins, but they're more like tiny homes. Each one is two stories, with a front door and window on the ground floor and a sliding glass door and balcony on the second floor. They're all painted the same snowy white, with unique artistic details in shades of beige and cream. Flowers, trees, animals, snowflakes, geometric designs. It reminds her of a row of wedding cakes in a baker's window.

"So what's the catch?"

As they walk, she can see in open doors and gleaming windows. They pass people painting, writing, sewing, reading in hanging chairs, curled over a desk inside, doing something that involves three curved computer monitors and a big set of headphones. All of these people, she notes, are *gorgeous*. Any one of them could be a movie star or model.

"There is no catch, but you're welcome to try to find one. Only one in ten of the people Jesper interviews are invited to stay. Some days, he wakes up with 'a feeling' and sends someone out, and there's inevitably some random act of chance that connects us with an artist who needs this place. Someone who, in turn, is needed here."

Solomon stops in front of a tiny house painted with snowflakes. It's so narrow that if she holds her arms out wide, Angelina could almost touch both walls.

"There's an NDA, but it's a lot less complex than you'd think. We have rules here—we have to. But if you agree, and if it sounds like something you'd like to be part of, this could be your home for as long as you want to stay. We call this grand experiment the House of Idyll. It will never, ever, cost you a single cent. You'll own whatever you make, and we'll help you make it." He opens the door, and she smells fresh paint and lavender—a bouquet sitting on a two-seater kitchen table, right beside a sleek laptop that looks brand new.

"There has to be a catch. How is this possible?" She walks inside, opens cabinets to reveal neat rows of spotless glasses and hand-thrown mugs.

Solomon leans against a steep set of half-stairs, half-ladder that leads to the second-floor bedroom, which is open but for a railing. "You know how you look at billionaires and wonder why they spend their money on stupid shit that doesn't make them happy when they could do literally anything they wanted

44

to? We used to talk about it all the time on the tour bus. Hell, in Manny's mom's minivan, back before we even got our first gig."

It has taken this long for Angelina to recognize Solomon as the bassist of Black Idyll, and she feels like an absolute ass—except that not recognizing him meant she didn't quite take him seriously, which honestly is probably better. When he was younger, in Black Idyll's heyday, he was a pudgy punk who kept his head shaved and was known for multiple facial piercings, none of which are currently in evidence.

"So we made a list of everything we wanted to do if we ever had that kind of money. And now we're doing it. If we never made another dollar, our investments would still grow exponentially. All we want is to make the world better, and part of that is finding struggling artists—people like we used to be—and giving them the helping hand we used to pray for. All you have to do is follow a few simple rules, make your art, grow as a human being, and try to improve the planet in your own unique way. Easy-peasy, lemon squeezy."

He points to a stapled packet on the table. "Read it. If you sign it, this place is yours for as long as you like. So is that laptop, by the way. The official Black Idyll Vantablack MacBook Air. Brand new. Set your own password. There's a group dinner at seven, but you can eat whenever you want. The kitchen is available to all, or you can eat here. Someone will come find you and tell you more."

"And if I don't sign it?"

Solomon regards her solemnly.

"Then we kill you."

Walking is a series of controlled falls
You want to run but you're too proud to
    crawl
You crave much more but you have
    it all
If you won't be silent, you can't hear
    the call
Say yes, say yes, undress, obsess
Throw yourself on my altar, say yes,
    confess

"NAKED & FAMOUS," BLACK IDYLL, TRACK #1 ON SEXY YOUNG GODS:
THE SEXY YOUNG SOUNDTRACK, KAKOPHONY RECORDS, 2017.

5

Angelina's jaw drops, and her hand fumbles for the phone in her back pocket.

Solomon throws back his beautiful head and laughs.

"Just kidding. Mr. B will take you back to LA, drop you off wherever you want. No harm, no foul." He shoves his hands in his pockets and chuckles. "No matter how many times I say that, watching people freak out never fails to amuse me."

"That's... kind of gross, actually," she mutters sourly.

"Newsflash, love: billionaire rock star playboy philanthropists are allowed to keep their twisted sense of humor. We're allowed to do pretty much anything we want, *actually*." He gives her the look of a mischievous little boy who knows he will never, ever get in trouble and winks. "Good thing I'm not a bad guy, huh? And that I'm trying to make all your dreams come true? Anyway, welcome." He brings his palms together and bows his head. "Namaste."

Hands back in his pockets, he glides toward the villa with

liquid grace. Angelina watches through the window, wondering if this is how the ancient Greeks felt about demigods. She has never been around someone ridiculously wealthy before, but she begins to understand why they all seem obsessed with going to Mars.

Now alone in the tiny house, she sits at the table, reading through the paperwork. She was expecting cramped, confusing legalese, but it's very straightforward and hinges more on her rights than on those of House of Idyll LLC. After three reads, she can't find a loophole, can't find some sneaky way they can claim her work or steal her rights. This really is legit—or so it seems. She opens the MacBook and goes through the quick motions of setting it up, then hops on the Wi-Fi and searches House of Idyll LLC. There's not a single controversy around it, not one black mark. Again and again, artists and writers and designers praise the hand up they received, heaping thanks and love upon Jesper, Solomon, Manny, and Nico.

Of course, when you have that kind of money, you can generally pay to bury bad press, but...

"Knock, knock."

Angelina looks up to find the driver—Mr. B?—smiling at her as he leans in the door.

"Didn't mean to startle you, sweetheart. You sign those papers yet? If not, I'm headed into the city now. Solomon said to take you home if that's where you're headed."

The pen is in Angelina's hand, the paperwork open to the signature page. Mr. B glances at his watch—a big, golden thing that looks like it cost more than her old apartment building.

"Don't mean to rush you, but it's now or never. Just follow your heart."

"Do you take many people back?" she asks.

"Just the dumb ones. Who would pass this up? Jeez." He steps inside, and she begins to wonder if he's a bouncer in addition to being a driver. Still, she doesn't find his presence threatening—although she could, under other circumstances. He's a big guy with a crooked nose and a gold tooth that suggests a rougher past. "Word to the wise. Sign the papers and stay. You won't get a chance like this again. Once in a lifetime." He nods sagely, hands on his hips, and she sees the gun snugly holstered against his ribs.

Is it a threat or an invitation?

She has maybe two minutes to decide the course of her life.

Does she take this lottery ticket with whatever cleverly hidden loophole is eluding her, or does she go back to a doomed life that will almost certainly lead to her calling her dad and tearfully begging for an airplane ticket back to nowhere?

You want to run but you're too proud to crawl, she thinks.

Just like the Line-A-Day calendar promised, there really is a Black Idyll lyric for every part of the human experience.

Following her gut, her heart, her fear, she signs the papers and holds them out. Mr. B takes them, inspects her signature, and nods his approval.

"Smart girl. I'll take these back to Mr. Solomon for you. Now all you have to do is make your dreams come true." He puts a fatherly hand on her shoulder, squeezes a little harder than necessary, and leaves.

Now all alone in a place that is... hers? All her very own? What?! She inspects every inch of the tiny home. She's starting to wonder about the details—what about her clothes? New underwear? Do they kick her out if she doesn't produce anything? Does she have to share her work with someone, prove she belongs here? None of that was in the paperwork.

Opening a narrow door, she uses the tiny house's tiny restroom, with its smart and tiny toilet and tiny shower and stack of fluffy white extra-large towels. Refillable soap, shampoo, and conditioner are affixed to the shower wall, with a bamboo comb and brush, a dental kit, a nail kit, and Idyllic-branded facial care and body lotion all neatly tucked away. There's even a box of unbleached, ethically sourced feminine hygiene products. It's nicer than the nicest hotel she's ever stayed in.

She climbs up the steep stairs to the comfy full-sized bed mounded with fluffy white pillows. The armoire beside it hosts white wooden coat hangers but no clothes. The drawers are likewise empty. Back downstairs, the little fridge contains only bottled water in 100 percent recycled aluminum bottles. The brand is, again, Idyllic, a special reverse-osmosis mineralized electrolyte spring water guaranteed to "raise your vibration." There is no TV. There is no food. It almost feels like the first level of a video game, like she has to go scavenge to begin building up the basics of a life.

"Hello?"

There's a girl in the doorway; she looks a lot like Kate Hudson in *Almost Famous*, dressed in all white.

"Hi, I'm Van," she says with a little wave. "You're new, right?"

"Yeah. Haven't even been here ten minutes. I'm Angelina."

Van smiles, showing dimples. "So you're in the 'what the hell have I done and where do I get underwear?' stage?"

Angelina exhales in relief to be so immediately understood. "Precisely."

"If you want to come on up to the Well, I'll show you how it all works."

Angelina considers her tote bag, which contains her wallet and laptop—old laptop, now—and her new MacBook. "They didn't give me a key. How do I lock up?"

The look Van gives her is knowing and indulgent. "You don't. When laptops are free and plentiful, you don't need to protect your laptop. You can twist the deadbolt from the inside while you're sleeping or whatever, but nobody has any keys. There's a little safe, though, if you need that. Like in a hotel. In the bottom of the closet upstairs."

Digging her wallet and old laptop out of her bag and feeling terribly self-conscious, Angelina pokes around until she finds the safe, which is hidden in a drawer. It works just like a safe in a hotel, and she feels better once she's stowed her things. Not that her wallet is particularly valuable—her bank account is currently in the double digits—but her ID is the sort of thing an actual cult would value. She sets the safe to her usual passcode and follows Van outside. It feels weird to leave the door unlocked, but... well, there's nothing to steal. How strange, to be in a land of plenty where people don't need to hoard resources.

Van is tall and willowy and walks with the swaying, hipless motion of a giraffe. Angelina keeps pace beside her, feeling small and grubby and like she stands out shockingly in this idyllic—no pun intended—paradise.

"So here's how it works," Van tells her, long white skirt swirling over her sandals. "The Well is the gathering place for meals, news, hanging out, critique sessions, meetings, whatever. Anyone can use it. Just sign out the meeting room you want. There's a kitchen that's open twenty-four-seven and meals at normal mealtimes. If you're a snacky person, you can take stuff back to your fridge, but they ask that you don't waste food. We do a lot of composting and use it to fertilize the gardens where we grow our veg. You can volunteer for that, too, if you like. It's all organic."

They're past the row of tiny homes now—wait, no. Two rows, staggered so everyone has a view of the forest. Then there's another big barn, painted white and wide open, but instead of fuzzy brown noses, she sees art studios with big can lights shining on enormous canvases, looms, tables covered with dusty clay. All the artists are, as she's beginning to expect, beautiful people dressed in white, although some of that white is splotched with paint or clay.

Heaven help whoever does laundry here.

Next they pass an enormous garden, bigger than an Olympic swimming pool and bursting with greenery. The people working within wear wide white sun hats, bobbing along the rows like flowers. Chickens peck around among the herbs, plump and shiny in a rainbow of colors. There are several greenhouses and many outbuildings and a fancy chicken coop bigger than Angelina's first apartment, plus a building that's made almost entirely of glass in which a yoga class is currently pursuing headstands.

"Are you sure this isn't a cult?" she asks.

Van doesn't laugh. "I know, right? Yoga and white clothes. Very Kundalini. I thought that for the entire first month. But... well, if you didn't have to go to some shit-ass job and take care of your kids or parents and pay bills, what would you want to do with your time? Most people want to make art and do yoga. There are also running trails, hiking trails into the forest, and a lake for swimming. Oh! And a gym. If there's something you want to do that will aid your health or personal growth, there's a suggestion box in the Well, and if enough people are interested, we can make it happen. And once a month, there's a personal empowerment seminar. They're incredible. Life changing. You just missed one."

They're approaching a building that doesn't quite match the rest of the compound. It's bigger and very new, three stories, all sleek lines and mirrored glass.

"So this is the Well. Cafeteria and kitchen on the ground floor through there, theater through there. Meeting rooms and gym on the second floor. Laundry and Outfitting on the top floor, which is where you need to go."

"I am so not dressed for this," Angelina mutters.

"No one is when they get here. I mean—come on. White? Unless you have a full staff that's immune to bleach, who would?"

They take a curving stairwell up to the third floor, and soon Angelina is shopping in what most resembles a Free People store, except everything is white cotton, white linen, white silk, white gauze. All natural fibers, all ideal for a photo shoot in a daisy meadow. Angelina adds white jeans and tees to her pack of white bikini undies and soft, stretchy bras, but Van tosses some skirts and loose dresses into her jute basket.

"You may not think you want them, but you will," Van says.

After Angelina has changed into a white tank and jeans with white sandals, she adds her old clothes to the basket, but Van stops her.

"Just toss them," she says, very serious, a hand on Angelina's arm.

"Do you know how hard it is to find jeans this soft that fit this well?"

There's an odd glow in Van's eyes. "You have to let go of your old life."

Angelina's hand tightens on the ratty jeans. "I thought you said this wasn't a cult."

"It's not. But the entire point is personal growth. Moving beyond. If you just hold on to all the same old shit, you can't really step off the cliff. You have to let go." She tugs on the jeans, and Angelina holds fast.

"This isn't a symbol. It's just jeans."

"Bestie, respectfully, everything is a symbol here."

Van's eyes flit to a corner, where Angelina spots the unblinking black eye of a camera. How many cameras are there in the compound, she wonders, and who watches them? The paperwork said she agreed to being on film, but she was more expecting selfies and video shoots with the band. She makes a show of opening her hand, releasing the jeans. Van pulls them and the wad of black shirt and old undies out of Angelina's basket and drops them in a trash can.

"There!" she says cheerfully. "Now you're set!"

"What about my stuff back home?" Angelina asks, not that she has much.

"They'll take care of it."

"Who?"

Van waves her hands through the air. "The band. Mr. B. Like I said, just... let go."

This makes Angelina feel distinctly untethered, but...

It's too late now, isn't it?

They stop in the kitchen for some basic groceries and snacks, and as Van packs everything into reusable net bags, Angelina realizes she doesn't know a single thing about the other woman.

"So how did you end up here?" she asks.

Van finishes artfully arranging apples and carrots and hummus in the bag before saying, "I'm a painter. I had a piece go viral, and I guess somehow Jesper saw it and contacted me to buy it. I thought it was some sort of scam—I mean, since when do rock stars slide into your DMs to ask the price of a painting? But there was the check mark, and he's the first client who hasn't tried to haggle me down. He asked if I would deliver it personally if he covered travel, and here I am. I've been here, maybe four months? And I got to be in a Black Idyll video, so that was cool."

As they walk back to Angelina's house—Angelina has a house!—Van introduces her to Lisbon and Marnie in the garden, Jorge riding past on a bike, Thierry out smoking something that is definitely not a cigarette with charcoal smears on the backs of his hands and a massive, ancient camera weighing down his neck. When he sees her, his gaze sharpens, and he snaps a picture for which she is entirely unprepared.

"Why is everyone so beautiful?" Angelina asks quietly.

"Because this place is all about beauty. Beauty and art and becoming. I guess, from one perspective, it seems a little..."

"Prejudiced?"

A birdlike shoulder rises in a shrug. "Not my money, not my business. I'm just glad to be here. Out of all the people in the world, we were chosen, you know? There's a serendipity to it. Millions of starving artists online, and a billionaire just so happened to fall in love with my painting of a unicorn right when I was trying to figure out how to break up with my boyfriend and move out. I'm not going to complain."

They're standing in front of Angelina's tiny home. Van walks inside like she's never heard of boundaries and places the net bags on the kitchen counter. "I'll stop by before dinner, if you like? We can go in together."

"Thanks. I'd like that."

With a flutter of white-painted fingernails, Van swirls away.

Finally alone again, Angelina sits at her table with a plate of hummus and carrots and checks her phone for the first time in hours. Lauren has sent multiple panicky texts, but Lisa and her parents have ignored her. She leaves her location share on and explains the situation in the group text.

Don't worry. I'm fine. You can see where I am. More later.

She doesn't fully understand what's happening herself, and now that she has some distance, she isn't sure that these people were ever her friends in the first place. Lisa is a favorite professor; Lauren is the person with whom she bitched about her boss. None of them have ever hung out.

With literally nothing else to do, she decides to get to work. She opens her new MacBook and transfers the files from her old laptop, which now looks like a blocky dinosaur, then pulls up her latest song on GarageBand. She's been working forty hours a week at the café and spending her nights catering to Crazy Barbara the Anti-Robot Tapioca Freak, which means she hasn't been able to work on her music for a couple of weeks.

It's a love song, but as she listens, her heart sinks. It's... lacking. Empty. Soulless. Angelina has never been in love, but every singer needs a love song. This is garbage. If Jesper Idyll knocked on her door right now and asked to listen, she would probably barf hummus on his bare feet.

She opens a new document and stares at the blank page.

What does she want to write? What is in her heart? What cliff is waiting to feel the grasp of her curling toes as she leaps? Why didn't she bring her goddamn guitar?

For her, it always starts with a melody, scratching at the back of her heart like a cat that wants inside.

When Van stops by to take her to dinner, the page is still blank—all white, just like everything else. Angelina asks if she can borrow an acoustic guitar, and Van says she'll ask around. She meets over thirty people that night, each prettier than the last, each happy and welcoming and full of good stories about what they've produced here. They gather and shift like kids in a high-school cafeteria. But over to one side is a long table with maybe a dozen people there, including the band. There is an aura around them, a golden glow.

"What's up with that table?" she asks Van.

Van looks over and rolls her eyes, but in a friendly way. "The Inner Circle. Kind of the leaders? Like, the band, and the people who teach the seminars. The ones who are already famous or well on their way. It's unofficially invite-only." She laughs. "God, I feel like I'm talking about the Cullens in *Twilight*. But I promise they're not vampires. And they're super nice. We just respect their space."

Watching the band chat with other vaguely famous, distractingly beautiful people, Angelina feels like a child, an idiot, a fraud. This is the big time, and she is not ready for the big time. She would not dare approach them. She should've washed her goddamn hair.

That night, with a belly full of veggie burger and fruit, she sits in the hanging chair on her balcony and stares up at the stars, trying to make sense of the constellations. The valley is vibrant with new sounds. Coyotes sing, frogs screech, bugs whine for sex, and somewhere, a violin trills like a ribbon dancer. The world opens up before her, fresh and new. Her entire life is a blank page. She can do anything, but what will she do?

She tosses and turns and dreams of a herd of pale horses running through the forest, their hooves pounding like thunder, as something chases them toward a cliff.

They gave you a castle
You made it a sty
The ugliest truth
Kills the prettiest lie
Plastic and saline and
   needles and wire
Can't stop time or save you
   when all is on fire

"20 DOLLAR BILL," TRACK #6 ON BLACK IDYLL,
(RE)HEARSE, KAKOPHONY RECORDS, 2014.

6

Angelina unwillingly wakes up at dawn. Something has pulled her from the velvety fist of sleep. Soft, lavender light filters in through the sheer white drapes over the balcony sliding glass door; she's going to ask if they have any blackout curtains or maybe an eye mask, because she suspects making up for years of sleep deficit will play a big role in her ability to write again. She rolls over, pulling the puffy white duvet over her head, and that's when she hears it: a gentle knock on her front door.

"No thank you," she mutters.

She rolls out of bed—the mattress is on a low platform—and fumbles down the stairs in her old-fashioned white nightgown like a confused ghost bumbling out of a Victorian attic. Hand on the doorknob, she takes a deep breath and tries to look like she's not fucking pissed to be awakened for dawn yoga or whatever the hell, but when she opens the door, it's not Van.

It's Jesper Idyll.

Standing there like the most beautiful phantom, gleaming white in the indigo strangeness, seeming to materialize from the forest.

"Walk with me," he says.

The reasons to say no tumble through her head: I'm sleeping, I'm not dressed, this is weird, I'm pretty sure you can see my nips through this muumuu, just because you're my teenage celebrity crush doesn't mean I trust you in the wilderness alone.

But she just slips on her sandals and steps outside, closing the door softly behind her.

Jesper moves like he has no physical weight, like his feet aren't touching the ground. He's wearing a slightly different white tunic and white pants set, and he's still barefoot. Without looking back, he walks into the forest, and something tugs at Angelina's memories—the dream of the horses running, screaming, and pawing, sweaty necks curved as they dodged the tree trunks. There's a path, but not much of one. Angelina walks behind Jesper, her eyes fading in and out of focus. The ends of his blond hair curl around his shoulder blades like a marble statue of a satyr.

She thinks back to everything she's said and experienced since she arrived. It hasn't even been twenty-four hours; has she done something so egregious that they're kicking her out? Is this because she didn't want to give up her jeans? Because she couldn't even write one word yesterday?

The forest is otherworldly in the predawn mist. Sculptures

of birds in flight hang from branches, and stumps have been carved into bears and rabbits and one teardrop-shaped raccoon. They pass hand-carved benches and even a treehouse with chicken legs that suggests Baba Yaga might summer here. It's magical and ethereal, a cottagecore Disneyland. Still Jesper remains silent, and while Angelina's general anxiety would typically cause her to speak up, to ask what she's done wrong, she senses that Jesper has no tolerance for that sort of desperation.

Finally the trail widens, spitting them out at a lake. It's massive, the water still, the far edges ringed by tufts of green grass, framed by an oddly rococo backdrop of scrubby golden hills limned in dawn's rosy glow. The surrounding area is rocky, but they've stubbornly created a manmade beach with sand stolen from an hourglass, pure and clean as sugar. Two Adirondack chairs are sunk in the field of soft white, and Jesper sits in one, looking out at the tiny ripples in the ink-black water. Angelina takes the other chair and tries to get comfortable.

"How are you settling in?" Jesper asks.

Time stretches out as she trawls her sleep-muddled brain for the right answer.

It feels like another test.

But everything in front of Jesper, she thinks, would feel like a test.

A fish jumps in the lake, making Angelina visibly startle.

"That's the hardest I've slept in years," she says, aiming for honesty that bypasses yesterday's terrifying introduction to writer's block. "It's so peaceful here."

Jesper nods, his head bobbing with the concentric rings wafting out from the fish's splash.

"You're frightened of me."

The words are not an accusation, but they are true, nevertheless.

"Not frightened. Intimidated. I'm sure you get that a lot."

Finally he looks at her, and recognition sparks behind her eyeballs, fizzes in her blood, tingles to every extremity. Being seen by Jesper Idyll is a full-body experience.

His smile is genuine, warm. "I do. At least you're not stuttering and kowtowing and telling me how much you love my work."

Angelina sends up a silent thanks to Lauren, who pulled her aside on her first day at the café after she couldn't stop staring at a B-level movie star to explain that the best way to get through life as a barista in Hollywood was to treat stars as if they were the most normal and boring people on the planet. No eye contact. No recognition. No secret smile. No subtle phone photos. And for God's sake, just use whatever fake name they give and never say their real name out loud.

"I can see how that would be uncomfortable to hear all the time."

"Then I'll only tell you this once, Angelina: I'm a fan of your work."

Is... he joking?

"What work?"

"I went through your Instagram. Your voice is incredible, and your songs are compelling. Bewitching. Like early Fiona

Apple. A little Stevie Nicks, a little Janis Joplin."

This must be what it's like to be struck by lightning. Angelina's fingers clench the arms of her chair, her body gone rigid with psychic shock. At no point did she think Jesper Idyll would take any sort of personal interest in her art. She thought yesterday's interview was a formality, like meeting with the college dean once before being summarily forgotten, just one in a sea of thousands.

"How—?" is all she can manage.

"House of Idyll owns a majority share of the coffee franchise where you worked. When Solomon decided to bring you in, we accessed their records and did a full background check, including a social media evaluation. Solomon saw a lot of promise in your music and passed it on to me. We don't let just anyone in, you know."

This is alarming and intrusive and yet... totally reasonable. She has been invited into what's basically a patron-funded creative think tank; it makes sense that they would look into her art and her history. Now she understands why they asked so few questions. They didn't *need* to ask questions. They already knew everything they needed to know.

Still, she would've preferred an actual interview to a secret, behind-the-scenes deep dive into her life.

"Thank you," she says evenly, but it sounds ridiculous, and he's got to notice.

"I'm just a person." Jesper's voice is so quiet she wonders if she imagined it. "This land—it's the one place where I should be able to live a normal life. Beyond these walls, I can't get a cup of coffee. Can't go to a movie. If I walk down the street of any city in the world, I'll be mobbed. Someone always sees through the disguise. But here, please, think of me as just a person. That's what I want."

He reaches over and puts his hand atop hers where it clutches the chair arm for dear life. His touch is firm, pressing. At first, it's awkward, but then she realizes what he's doing.

"Are you grounding me? Calming me down like a race-horse? Are you my goat?"

The laugh erupts from him, very real and raucous—not acting, not controlled.

A real laugh.

"Yes, Angelina, I'm the goat to your thoroughbred. Or maybe the opposite. It takes people a while to get used to me. That's why I bought this place, originally. I needed a playground I could build to my specifications. A place where I could be myself."

"I—"

"Shh."

She senses a tension in him, an immediacy. He stares out over the lake, sculpted brows drawn down over serious eyes as deep as the water beyond. His finger taps against the back of her hand, keeping time. She is utterly silent. An artist always recognizes the look of inspiration striking.

> *Bred for beauty, bred to run.*
> *Champions can't have any fun.*
> *Built for power, trained for might.*

The boxer can't escape the fight.
Every racehorse needs a goat,
A drowning man must love the boat.

His voice is heartbreakingly beautiful as he sings each line, and Angelina realizes she is watching genius at play. She holds her breath until the last syllable. Jesper looks to her, his eyes on fire.

"No notes," she whispers.

He stands and falls to his knees before her, taking her hand from the chair and kissing it, courtly as a knight.

"Thank you," he tells her, looking deep into her eyes with abject gratitude.

Angelina is flustered, smitten, twitterpated, charmed, overcome, probably honestly almost kinda really having a panic attack, her heart knocking around in her chest like a thirsty hummingbird.

"Any time."

Jesper releases her hand and stands. "I guess it's the studio for me today. I'll shoot over a rough draft when I'm done. Let me know what you think." He pauses. "But only if you promise to be honest. Pretty lies are useless to me."

"'The ugliest truth kills the prettiest lie,'" she says, then blushes. Did she really just recite his own song lyrics to him like an absolute teenybopper idiot?

But he just chuckles. "It's hard to revisit old art, but I stand by that line. Welcome, Angelina. I can tell you're going to blossom here."

He does the same namaste bow that Solomon did yesterday and is swallowed by the welcoming maw of the wood. Angelina can't wait to return to her little house and go back to sleep for a few more hours, but it would be horribly awkward to be stalking Jesper Idyll through the forest like some kind of freak, especially when he's just explained how much he hates that sort of thing. Instead, she sits back in her chair, forcing herself to enjoy the beauty of the sun rising over the—well, it's actually rising behind her, but still. The rolling hills ripple with pinks and purples, the flat lake reflecting nature's paintbrush. Angelina can't remember the last time she watched the sun rise. She can't remember the last time she was able to pause and pay attention to her physical existence, to let it fill up her senses. Ever since her parents cut her off, her life has been a desperate fight to stay afloat. Much like the racehorse in her earlier metaphor, she has worn blinders in order to focus on what mattered most. Suddenly her vision has widened, and she's seeing colors and nuance that have been missing from her life. The world is a panorama instead of a dark tunnel.

Far off, she hears a horse's whinny and wonders if she's imagined it, conjured it, if Jesper Idyll's pull on her imagination is so strong that—

But no. On the far side of the lake, a small herd of horses meanders over a hill, tails swishing, and crowds close at the water's edge to drink. They're far away and shifty, their hides all but blending in with the golden shimmer of the rising sun. Grays and palominos and duns. One achingly white horse stands on the crest of the hill, keeping watch, his mane and tail blowing in a breeze.

She sees him, and he sees her. He raises his head and bugles.

She can't tell if it's a warning or a welcome.

She raises one hand, and the horse stamps and rears, spinning in place. He runs to the other horses, snaking his head to hurry them away from the water. They squeal and stampede, knocking into one another as they run like hell back into the hills.

Angelina looks at her hand. Surely these wild horses weren't frightened of her?

A cold chill runs down her back.

She stands and looks at the forest behind her.

Or were they scared of something else?

Bred for beauty, bred to run
Champions can't have any fun
Built for power, trained for might
The boxer can't escape the fight
Every racehorse needs a goat
A drowning man must love the boat
Fall to your knees and kiss the feet
That saved you from becoming meat.

"SAVE ME FROM MYSELF," UNRELEASED.
FROM THE PRIVATE COLLECTION OF JESPER IDYLL.

7

There is nothing hiding among the trees; nothing she can sense, anyway. The forest was shadowy and strange when she walked through it with Jesper, but now that the sun is up, it's easy to see between the trees. She wonders if this is grizzly country, or if maybe they're far enough out that mountain lions still roam. The horses fear something besides her; she knows that much for certain. She'll have to ask Van about the local fauna later. She went through a Horse Girl phase in elementary school and learned everything she could from books, but her hands-on experience is embarrassingly non-existent. Unsupportive parents are rarely willing to pay the money it takes to be around horses.

As she stands, staring into the forest, looking for movement, a shiver crackles over her skin. The sky is going dark, heavy black clouds moving in with the impersonal fury of an avalanche. The temperature falls like a dropped glass, and the hairs rise on Angelina's arms.

"Shit," she mutters, hurrying toward the forest path.

Even if Jesper isn't yet in the studio, surely he would understand that she's not following to swoon over him; she's trying to escape being struck by lightning in a freak storm, the kind she has never seen a single time since moving to California. A rumble permeates the air, the ground shivering under her sandals. The leaves on the trees shake in warning or fear. She struggles to find the path; it was clear when she walked behind Jesper, even though it was darker then.

Or so she thought. As the clouds bear down, it might as well be full-on night.

That's when she feels the first raindrops strike.

Because they do not fall or plunk or tumble or thump.

Each one slams down like a slap of reproof, heavy and sharp.

She's jogging now, wishing she wasn't in a light, filmy gown and the thinnest of sandals. Has she even seen an umbrella since she got here—since she's been in California? No. It barely drizzled one day, and every single person who walked into the café remarked upon it with the same gravity they gave to the eclipse. A rare, strange thing worth the annoyance.

Crash!

White light blinds her. The ground jerks under her feet, and she stumbles.

That was close.

Too close.

She picks up the pace, running past the hanging bird sculptures that seemed so joyful and bright when she walked with Jesper, but now they shake and dance like bat puppets come to life, jerked about by the wind tugging the branches and ripping off their leaves. The sculpted stumps rise up like trolls clutching for her skirts—why the fuck is she wearing this stupid nightgown?—and she rips it free from a carved bear's imagined claws and gives the next stump a wide berth.

Another burst of light, another crash of lightning meeting earth.

It strikes a tree this time, splitting the trunk in half with a scream of protest, peeling it down in two parts, its raised branches all too similar to a woman's arms falling gracefully as she's ripped in half. The acrid burn of fire smacks Angelina in the face, and she runs as fast as she can, ignoring everything except the path before her.

She's soaked now, the white nightgown plastered to her like a caul, her hair matted down over her eyes. The sandals fly off into the forest, sacrificed for speed. Her feet are so cold she doesn't feel any pain. The wind whips the trees back and forth; they're nearly doubled down to the earth, their branches arching like black rainbows. Angelina sees the end of the trail up ahead and puts on an extra burst of speed. She explodes from the forest and sprints to her tiny home. There's so much rain that she can barely see. It slashes sideways, pelting her from every direction, filling her eyes. Finally her hand closes on the doorknob, and she throws herself inside and slams the door behind her, twisting the deadbolt as if she's being chased.

For a long moment, she can only stand there, soaked, dripping on the gray floor. The sound of the thunder and cracking lightning is muffled now, but this place offers little safety. She whips her torn nightgown over her head and goes directly into the shower, turning the water to hot and panting as she waits for it to warm up. She wants to wash this storm off her skin, to feel clean and soft again. When she steps into the narrow cubicle, the warm water is luscious as it caresses her body, so unlike the hateful slap of the rain. The Idyllic bath products fill the room with the glorious perfume of white flowers, cool and gentle and reassuring. The mud and leaves are scoured from her legs and feet, the dirty water nearly black. Once it flows clear, she notices blood; the soles of her feet are scratched and cut. Once she's thoroughly clean, she just stands there with the water flowing down her back, regaining her sense of calm.

The hot water doesn't last long; she must have her own small water heater. She dries off with a fluffy white towel and wraps it around her body for the awkward stair climb up to her wardrobe. Whoever planned these little houses clearly didn't realize that the closet would be better off downstairs. She slips into another nightgown, identical to the wet one wadded up on the floor, and climbs back into bed. Let the storm rage. Inside, it is dark and still and safe. The rain pounding on the roof lulls her back to sleep.

In that liminal space between dream and reality, a song begins to coalesce. Something real and meaty and deep and tragic and beautiful, the kind of thing she used to write before she was forced to hammer her round passion into the square hole of a money-making social media venture. She feels her soul coming alive like a banked fire fed human breath, little puffs to bring sleeping coals back to their original heated fury.

It is a love song, she thinks, and Jesper Idyll is the object of exquisite yearning.

She reaches for her laptop, opens a new document— because yesterday's document is ruined, lacking, failed. She starts typing lyrics in bits and pieces, catches the chorus like butterflies in a net. She finds the shape of it, the blind man running hands over an elephant, and for the first time in forever, she feels the beautiful kiss of obsession.

Then she falls back asleep, a lover spent.

Thankfully, she is allowed to sleep as long as she likes. This is an unusual gift, but it is not the only gift. Along with a nice microphone, and a set of headphones, an acoustic guitar is waiting in a case on her kitchen table. A Martin, which she never dreamed she might touch, much less own. It's brand new with all the accessories and a strap. Top of the line.

The color, of course, is white.

She is immediately smitten, stunned, in awe. She delights in the heft of it, traces its curves, plucks out the first notes of her new song and feels excitement trill up her spine at the perfection of the mellow sound. Only when she opens her door to head to the Well for breakfast does she realize that her door is unlocked. Did she leave it that way, or did her fairy guitar-father forget? And... does someone else have a key, because she certainly doesn't. Maybe she's not worried about theft, but she she's fairly certain she engaged the deadbolt before going back to sleep... and yet someone has been here. Inside.

While she was unconscious.

Which is... worrisome.

Outside, the world is sunny and bright, water droplets sparkling on every surface like glitter after an opulent party. The sky is deep azure and the sun is shining double time as if in aggressive apology, nearly blinding where it glances off all the glass. Angelina doesn't see any people, which she finds surprising, but maybe they're very California people and the thought of rain is foreign. When she gets to the garden, she finds it empty, and she's drawn under the twining arbor and into a riot of sights and smells. She doesn't know much about plants, but she can feel the energy brought by the rain, the way every little leaf has perked up at attention. Bees and butterflies cluster on flowering bushes, while shiny vegetables wink from the dappled shadows. Angelina doesn't dare pick anything; this is not her place, and although she feels welcome, she does not feel ownership. Maybe she'll ask for a shift working here. Maybe they'll teach her the names of each plant, let her twist a dewy pepper from its stem.

The garden is even larger than it seems from the outside, seemingly chaotic but following a perfect Fibonacci spiral like a snail's shell. Angelina has passed flowers, herbs, vegetables, even an empty bed full of rich, black soil with tiny sprouts planted in neat rows, glistening with the recent rain. As she approaches the center of the garden, she realizes that there's a gazebo there, nearly hidden by vines and flowering bushes. She angles for the structure, thinking it might be a nice place to bring her laptop and write, once everything is dry again—if there's a bench and plenty of shade.

It takes a moment to find the entrance, thanks to the wild overgrowth of greenery. But once Angelina stands before it, she immediately knows something is wrong. There's an odd stillness, as if the wind isn't touching the trumpet flowers twined over the white lattice. The shade within is cool and dark. Something is lumped there on the floor of the gazebo, an odd but organic shape.

Stepping closer, Angelina sees that it is a white chicken.

And it is dead.

In the garden of Eden, no crime occurred
The line between innocence and arrogance
    was blurred
We ended up naked but started out furred
Eve didn't feign hunger when Adam demurred
Ignorance, a barbed-wire fence
Set me up for failure and shit'll get tense

"TRUST THE SNAKE," TRACK #4 ON BLACK IDYLL, NEVER
RHYME FRIEND WITH END, KAKOPHONY RECORDS, 2016.

8

Angelina is not squeamish. She is not the sort to tear at her hair and scream, to swoon in a faint and cry. She is a writer. She is curious. She is morbid. She cares about details.

She steps closer, trying to puzzle out the grisly scene.

The poor chicken's head is separate from its body, lying a little bit away. There is no knife, no clear weapon. She wonders if maybe it was a predator, except a predator would've eaten the chicken — and left a mess of blood and feathers. Aside from the fact that her head is two feet away from her body and there's not a drop of blood anywhere, the hen seems perfectly normal. An animal wouldn't do this. A human would, but why?

Angelina feels as if she has trespassed on something she was not meant to see. Walking backward, feet squelching in wet gravel, she exits the center of the garden and hurries past jolly red peppers and gleaming eggplants on her way to the Well. The building is oddly empty. She helps herself to a mug of coffee from a large silver urn, stirs in stevia and Idyllic brand neurotropic, dairy-free creamer. Until she arrived here, she had no idea how far this—company? brand?—had penetrated society. Then again, she's poor. She doesn't buy things that contain fancy mushrooms and MCT oil. She has trouble believing that paying extra for organic is going to save her from cancer and extend her life when her blood is already brimming with microplastics. She doesn't care if the bagel is made from Himalayan wheat if it will keep her alive, but she does pause to read the tiny writing on the butter tub.

Idyllic believes in small farms and the people who have tended the land for generations, the shiny gold foil reads. We believe that health is happiness, and that beauty is born at the cellular level. Scan the QR code to see where your butter began.

Angelina scans the QR code and learns that the butter came from a heifer named Beatrice who lives in Wisconsin. There's even a picture of a soft brown cow with kind eyes.

"It's got to be a cult," she murmurs to herself.

Van meets her at the door looking like a kid on Christmas morning. "I've been looking for you. Come on! Nico is teaching a class."

Nico.

The drummer of Black Idyll.

"OK. Do I have time to finish my coffee?"

Van grimaces, showing bright white veneers. "You should definitely not drink coffee before doing hot yoga." She looks Angelina up and down and reaches to take the coffee and bagel from her. "Run upstairs and grab some yoga stuff. I'll wait. Hurry!"

There are approximately three million things Angelina would rather do than attempt hot yoga. She has never done hot yoga before. She doesn't like being hot, and she doesn't really enjoy yoga. But she wants to fit in, and she wants to be liked, and she wants to stay here in this bizarre, life-changing paradise, and so she runs upstairs, trades her white jeans and tee for a new pair of white yoga pants and a complicated white athletic bra that looks like a game of cat's cradle, and joins Van, who has poured her coffee down the sink.

They walk to the building with all the windows, and there are at least thirty people in the big room, laying out white yoga mats in neat rows on the glowing wood floors beside white towels and silver water bottles. An excited quiet blankets the space as people nod to each other, place their phones and bags into cubbies, and give the namaste bow. Angelina is startled to notice an up-and-coming singer who's on several of her playlists, a young actress who stunned at her first Met Gala last year, and a charismatic personal chef with a man bun she saw on a cooking competition—all gorgeous, of course, and all clad in white. Their eagerness and general glow are contagious, and she wishes she'd had time to brush out her hair and maybe add some waterproof mascara and lip stain. Van hands her a mat, and they take places against the wall. There are three mats laid out near the front, and Angelina is not surprised when Jesper, Solomon, and the fourth band member, Manny, appear to claim them. There was once a fifth member of Black Idyll, Vivian, but she died the year before the band hit it big.

A strange but beautiful noise makes every head turn

toward the front of the room, where Nico is running a glass wand around a crystal bowl. Nico Ioannou is just as jaw-droppingly gorgeous as he was in the posters on Angelina's teen wall. He looks like Hercules from the Disney movie made flesh and poured into white bicycle shorts, his curly mop of hair the sun-kissed gold of beeswax and his skin a uniform tan that makes his bright green eyes all the more captivating. He has to be at least thirty, but he looks twenty, tall and lithe with elegant muscles decorated with tattoos and the proud, shiny pink scar from a sniper's bullet. Angelina hates that he—and all of Black Idyll, really—will have the opportunity to watch her make an absolute fool of herself on the mat.

Only then does she notice that the room is weirdly warm, the air thick with a woody incense she can't quite place. Nico welcomes them and takes his place at the front of his mat, sitting back on his knees. The room, as one, copies this pose, and he begins chanting. Angelina has no idea what he's saying, but it's easy enough to repeat the same nonsense phrase over and over, almost running out of breath before drawing in a lungful of hot air and chanting again. Time stretches out strangely, the words an infinite loop, and when they finish on a long hum of the word Om, Angelina feels almost bereft at the silence.

Now Nico stands, and everyone mirrors his movements perfectly as he leads the group through a series of sun saluta-tions. Before, Angelina has found yoga boring and struggled to hold poses, but something about the chanting, the heat, the incense, and Nico's gravelly voice make it easy for her to obey.

Her body feels open, receptive, ready to move and stretch. She is pliant and breathing fire, matching Nico's inhales and exhales. Her head grows light, as if it might float off like a balloon.

There is an exhilarating peace in being one of many, moving in tandem, tuned in to a frequency that makes Angelina feel like a humming bee in a busy, happy hive. Nico talks about peace, beauty, passion, surrender. With some poses, he encourages them to meditate. He tells them that hip openers can bring up new emotions, and as Angelina pushes her knees down and folds forward over her lap, tears drip from her nose to her mat. She is not the only one. Every heart here is in the process of opening, unfolding, blooming, becoming. Like leaves turned up to willingly embrace the approaching rain, they face Nico, their current sun, and raise their arms to the heavens.

She is a tree. She is a mountain. She is a peaceful warrior.

She greets the sun and bends to honor it.

She realizes that the soft music that has been playing in the background all along is entirely composed of Black Idyll songs translated into flutes and bells.

This is good. Her brain likes that. It is familiar yet new, washed clean of the rage and violence in Jesper's voice and Nico's drumming.

They move into the final pose, the one that serves as a practice for death. Angelina is on her back, arms at her sides, legs splayed. She melts into the floor, her limbs leaden. The ceiling overhead is a sea of white nothingness. Nico appears, smiling at her upside down, and places a cold, wet cloth over her eyes, forcing them to close. It smells of mint, and she smiles but knows better than to speak and thank him. She is a corpse. An empty, heavy, happy corpse, melting into the earth.

"Namaste," Nico finally says. "Thank you for sharing this time with me. Drum circle Friday night at dusk by the lake, if you're into that."

As if a spell has broken, all the corpses surrounding Angelina in the rich, dark soil come alive like little chubby grubs awakening in the darkness. They twitch and turn and scrape, and then the cloth falls from her eyes and she's wiggling her toes and rolling onto her side, reborn. The world is bleary, and she wants to go back to the chanting, the opening, the death.

"Great class, right?" someone says beside her.

It takes a few seconds for Angelina's brain to come back online.

Van. This beautiful angel is a girl named Van.

"Amazing," Angelina agrees. "I've actually never enjoyed yoga before literally right this moment."

Van throws back her beautiful head and laughs, showing a long, elegant throat. Everything is more beautiful now, more tender and pure and true.

"Nico's a really good teacher. It's like he took Kundalini and made it... better. Plus no turbans. I hate how I look in a turban."

Van shows Angelina how to spray off her mat and wipe it clean, and they drop their mint-soaked cloths in a white can, collect their belongings, and bow to Nico as they leave. Jesper, Solomon, and Manny are already gone. Thierry calls to Van, and they join a small circle for lunch at the Well. It's sushi, and it's light and delicious. Angelina has had sushi plenty of times before, but her taste buds are awake now, and she is astounded at the velvety fattiness of the fish, the slight acid of the rice, the umami of the soy sauce.

"First bliss, huh?" a dark-skinned girl named Kierra with an impressive cloud of natural hair says, smirking at Angelina.

"That's definitely not how my last yoga class went," Angelina admits. "Like, a lot less grunting in general. Is it always like that?"

"If Nico's teaching, yes. It's almost as if his pixie dust rubs off on you? Plenty of people teach classes, but everybody shows up for the Nico Special. It's like..."

"You go somewhere else," Thierry finishes for her. "Like flow, but you're invigorated afterward instead of drained." He focuses on Angelina. "So what do you do?"

Thierry has a slight French accent and a mustache that only works on extremely handsome, timeless men. If a guy like that spoke to Angelina out in the real world, she'd get all flustered, but here, all the men are so handsome that beauty loses its impact. He's not nearly as scary as Jesper Idyll; she knows that much.

"Singer-songwriter. I've been trying to make it happen on social media, but..." It's barely been twenty-four hours, but it's like she's an entirely different person, her old self a shed skin that she now finds slightly embarrassing. "I guess I've been stalled out. But I had an idea this morning, and it's got me by the throat."

Thierry laughs. "This place—it's like that. It acts on your

dreams. There's an energy, a vitality. It's like nothing else. Do you—"

Every head turns to stare at the door. Jesper has just walked in, following an ethereally beautiful woman who walks like she's dancing. Burnished tan skin, ink-black hair to the small of her back, white dress billowing around sun-kissed shoulders; she must be Miss Brazil, or Miss World, or Miss Something Better Than Everyone Else. Just as quickly as heads turned, they refocus on their food. Angelina doesn't look away fast enough, and Van taps her arm and shakes her head. Angelina shoves a random piece of sushi in her mouth and watches out of the corner of her eye as Jesper picks up two boxes of sushi and leads the mysterious woman up the stairs.

Once they've disappeared, Van says, quietly, "Maria Perez. Principal dancer in the Cuban Ballet. Jesper's current favorite."

She puts an emphasis on "favorite" that sounds like a verbal eyeroll.

"Favorite what?" Angelina asks.

"Favorite person," says Van.

Kierra stabs reproachfully at her sushi. "Favorite *anything*."

Thierry sighs. "There's always someone. He gets serially hyper-fixated. His dick has ADHD."

Angelina thinks back to the string of actresses and musicians he dated, back when she kept up with that sort of thing as a lovesick bi girl in high school. He stayed with another lead singer for maybe three years, once? But otherwise, he bounced around—and always had lots of fodder for love songs and tragic tales of heartbreak.

They go back to eating and chatting, but the post-yoga high has deteriorated. Angelina knows now what it feels like, to be alone with Jesper or have Nico's full attention, even for a few, brief moments. Maybe here, in this valley, they get to be regular people instead of world-renowned rock star millionaires, but it's clear that their star power remains intact, some sort of fundamental charisma that pulls people to them. Angelina once saw a field of sunflowers all facing the sun. It's like that, maybe. A desperate longing to be in that spotlight for as long as possible. She wants to ask if Jesper takes everyone for a walk when they first arrive, but she doesn't want people to look at her the way they looked at Maria, with a sort of jealous resentment. And she also doesn't want to hear that it's a universal treat and she's not actually special at all.

Once she's done poking at her sushi, she returns to her tiny home, showers off the yoga sweat, and slips back into jeans and a tank, energized to pick out the notes on her new guitar. When she opens her laptop to get started, she finds a message from Jesper Idyll. It's titled "Save Me From Myself," and at first, she panics, wondering if he's in some kind of trouble—

But no. It's the title of a song.

The email contains a link to a music-sharing site.

The track isn't perfect, isn't the sort of thing she's used to hearing from Black Idyll. They often play with a full orchestra, or at least with all four band members, and Jesper generally layers in multiple vocal tracks and additional instruments. Their songs are slick, heavily produced, commercial. Their songs are perfect.

But this is rough, breathy, quiet, personal.
This is Jesper alone with a guitar, picking out the notes—
Just like she's doing with her new guitar.

> *Every racehorse needs a goat*
> *A drowning man must love the boat*

Jesus Christ, he used her idea—
Jesper Idyll used her idea!
For a song!
It's like he's singing just for her.
The words in the email make Angelina's heart stutter.

> Thank you for this gift. I probably shouldn't have
> sent it, but I wanted you to hear it first. I trust you.
> xo, Jesper

In the darkest part of the darkest night
He wakes and walks in the fire's light
Why do you keep hidden, I want to ask
Why do you wear that human mask?

"SLEEP NO MORE," TRACK #1 ON BLACK IDYLL, THE
SUCCULENT REAPING, KAKOPHONY RECORDS, 2024.

9

Angelina is torn.

She wants to tell everyone she has ever met about this miracle.

She wants to send a massive *NEENER NEENER* text to everyone who thought she was a dork in high school, and to everyone who thought she was a failure in college, and to all her professors who didn't bother to learn her name, and tell them that a silly little metaphor she came up with while half asleep might soon be the basis for an official Black Idyll song.

She also wants to put the song on a thumb drive and swallow it in one gulp so that no one else will ever know about it and it will be a secret she keeps with Jesper Idyll forever.

Ultimately she does neither of those things.

As she's listening to it for the fifth time, it stops playing. It disappears.

The song has been removed.

She wasn't able to save it on her computer—she thought it

would just be there for her to enjoy—but now it's gone. If the email wasn't still there, she would think she'd imagined it.

If only she'd taken a video or—

Damn.

What a strange and fleeting joy.

Maybe one day she'll hear the finished version.

But the tune—it snags claws in her mind. She takes out her new guitar and plucks out the melody. Her version is more her style, and the lyrics come hard and fast, a counterpoint to Jesper's words. He wrote of being a drowning man; she writes of being the boat, the safe harbor, the comfort to someone perpetually unmoored.

> *Perhaps the goat was born to stand*
> *Beside the racehorse, hand in hand*
> *Hoof to hoof and heart to heart*
> *Til the gun goes off and the real race starts*

She writes like she's being chased, like the words are flowing into her blood, filling her body, a dusty, desiccated reservoir burgeoning with refreshing life. Like it's exactly what she was meant to do and to do anything else would be blasphemy. Like she's just a conduit for words pouring out of—

The muse, the ether, WHATEVER.

It is glorious, and she feels full and resplendent and shiny.

That feeling—

It keeps going.

She eats and sleeps as if in a fever dream. She forgets what the world sounds like without headphones. Van shows up with little gifts, sushi and muffins and tea with honey, reminding her that she's a person. Days later, although it honestly feels like hours, she looks up from the screen and is surprised to find that she exists in corporeal space. Her back and neck and fingertips ache, her feet are nearly asleep. The song is, she thinks, as perfect as she can make it using only the nicest guitar and tabletop equipment that money can buy. She has sung it repeatedly, recorded it, remixed it, added harmony. The sun is going down, the day caught in that strange, crepuscular moment of neither and both. She feels as if she is waking up from the deepest sleep of her life.

For the first time in years, she has produced something *real*. Her words, her voice, her soul, perfectly melded. Before she can think too hard about the implications of what she's doing, she sends the file to Jesper Idyll, replying to his email.

Reality falls like a curtain; what has she done?

She wrote a song and sent it to her idol, some would say the biggest rock star in the world.

Too late. What's done is done.

It's just another cliff, and maybe she'll break her neck, but it was one hell of a swan dive.

After a good stretch and a much-needed shower, she walks over to the Well, hoping to find some friendly dinner. There is only one other person there, a gorgeous Korean woman with huge eyes and a perfect pixie cut. The woman looks up and smiles when Angelina pauses by the buffet line with her tray. Angelina smiles back, makes the universal gesture for, "Can I sit with you?", and takes her seat.

"I'm Ji," the girl says.

"I'm Angelina. Are you new?"

"Very new. To be honest, I've been hiding in my house. I finally came out tonight, and no one is here." She sighs and pokes at her salad. "There is a girl named Van who has been very welcoming, but she's not at home. Or here. Where is everyone?"

Something plucks at Angelina's mind.

"What day is it?"

Ji cocks her head. "Friday."

"Friday. Really? Oh! There's a drum circle at seven." She checks her phone. It's a little after eight. "So I guess it's still going on."

"A drum circle?"

She didn't hear it before, but now that she's straining, there's a deep thumping somewhere far off, like the heartbeat of the world softly pounding. She's starving, but she's also curious.

"I think people just bring drums and sit around in a circle and play together, but I've never seen one before. Want to go?"

Ji looks at her salad, then the door. "I don't think so. Too many people."

Angelina considers her. She's beautiful, like everyone here, late teens or early twenties. "What do you do?"

At that, Ji smiles shyly, although eye contact is definitely not her thing. "Violin. I sent an audition tape to play for a Black Idyll song, and they invited me here. I can't do concerts, but I like recording studios. They want me to play on their next album."

A fierce jealousy spreads through Angelina like a cat's claws unsheathing. She wants to be in that recording studio. What would it feel like to sing into a microphone beside Jesper, to breathe in time with him and feel their voices meld?

"I think I'm going to go." She stands up, her dinner half eaten, and clears her tray.

"Will you be here for meals tomorrow?" Ji asks. "It would be nice to know someone."

Angelina smiles. "Probably. I'm in the snowflake house in the front row if you want to stop by. Nice to meet you!"

And then she's gone, headed home to freshen up. She's had her hair in a messy bun while writing, but now she lets it down and brushes it out into smooth waves. She puts on a white tank and long skirt and her sandals. She's starting to understand why they dress this way; she feels light and breezy and open. In her usual life, she generally dresses for safety first, then to hide stains or sweat, then to accentuate her body. Jeans are her staple, with a variety of black and gray tees and tanks, plus hoodies or sweaters in the winter. She wears sturdy boots that will last a long time and protect her feet or Chucks for walking and work.

But here, her priorities are different. She is always safe. She's not going to get mugged or attacked, will not need to run away from an active shooter or catcaller. As for stains, when everyone wears white and someone else does the laundry, that becomes less of a problem. The filmy skirt feels delicious as she walks outside, swirling with each step, and the sandals make her feel like she's on vacation.

As she sets foot on the forest path, she remembers the strange visions from her first morning here, the odd dreams and screaming horses and pounding rain. It's so hard to remember what a storm feels like when every day is sunny. She is a different person now. A singer with a melody caught in her hair, an artist open to the world like one big antenna. The storm was frightening, but it was also exciting. It woke her up, made her feel again. And then it lulled her into a liminal state, opened the aperture through which the muse finally danced back in. The forest feels more friendly and welcoming now, and she can see stars twinkling through the trees, more stars than she's ever seen before in her life.

The drums thrum, primal and guttural, the earth throbbing against the arches of her feet. The two chairs are gone from the soft white sand by the lake, replaced by a metal fire pit. Shadows pulse around the capering flames, people standing and sitting with drums between their knees. Some use the flats of their hands, some use sticks or paddles. No one is leading, but everyone is following.

Angelina stops just outside the fire's light. She is uncertain how to proceed. There's Nico with a pair of bongos, eyes closed and face glowing with sweat and firelight. There's Van and Thierry and Lisbon and Marnie and Kierra and two dozen strangers, all either playing the drums or dancing to their rhythm. Maria Perez, wearing only a white triangle bikini top and a white tutu, pirouettes on her own, one of the greatest ballerinas in the entire world giving a private performance in the middle of nowhere, her gold-braceleted bare feet coated in white sand. The flames dance playfully with her, reflecting on glimmering hair and spinning tulle and laughing lips. They could be cavemen, Angelina thinks. This could be any moment from the past two hundred thousand years, people coming together around a fire to make noise and move their bodies, a song older than time.

Van steps in front of her, a golden angel, all blue eyes and white teeth. She takes Angelina's hands and tries to pull her into the dance, but Angelina... can't.

She doesn't know what to do.

She is an observer, a flâneur, not a ballerina.

Who is she, to dance in a circle with Maria Perez?

"Come join," Van says. Her pupils are huge, her cheeks ruddy.

"I don't dance."

"Then come drink, and we'll change that."

Van leads her away from the fire to a collection of dark bottles nestled in the sand. She lifts one, and the glass is rimed in beads of condensation. The cork offers some resistance, but then the bottle is against Angelina's lips. She thought it was red wine, but it's... something else. Sangria, maybe? With something herbal, something floral, and underneath it all, the velvety bite of tannins. Angelina has never been one for red wine but is eager to feel less like an outsider and more like she did while singing with her headphones on, as if the world is finally the right size. She wants to be swept away into something bigger, taken back to a place where she has forgotten all her insecurities and fears. Yoga made her feel like one part of a larger animal, and she longs to regain that closeness.

"Whoa, tiger!" Van takes the bottle from her, and Angelina wipes red liquid from the corners of her mouth.

A cavern opens in her belly, hot as a pool of wax and just as thick and sticky. This time, when Van takes her hands, Angelina has no choice but to allow herself to be tugged along. They slip between two drummers and close enough to the fire that Angelina can feel the heat against her cheeks. Van has sweat through her tank top. She's not wearing a bra. She doesn't seem to care, and Angelina decides she doesn't care either. This place—she will give in to it fully. Everything that has happened so far has been a miracle. She will take every miracle that she can get. She will open herself up to it, let it seep into her pores, swallow it whole.

Maria Perez pirouettes past them, and then Angelina is spinning, her white skirt twirling around her. She is a flower, a butterfly, a tornado. Her heart is a drum; the drums command her heart. Her feet know what to do. The world is a gorgeous, glorious blur. Maria takes her hands in fingers as light as bird bones and raises their arms and lifts her leg over her head, using Angelina to create geometry with her curving spine before leaping away again. Angelina sways, alone, lost, until someone catches her, pulls her close, and she rejoices at the heat of another animal lost in the dance.

It's Van. Beautiful, golden Van. Her skirt has slipped down her hips, and her lips are open and stained red.

"Can I kiss you?" she asks, but she doesn't wait for an answer. She shoves her fingers into Angelina's hair and pulls her face close, and she's as hot as the fire, burning, melding, golden, melted, honey dripping between them, slipping from her lips, a tongue slicking across Angelina's teeth like a fox lapping at blood—

"No."

Van pulls away.

Jesper Idyll stands there, his eyes so light they are almost white, his cornsilk hair coiling like albino snakes around his shoulders. He wears no shirt, and his chest is carved of wet alabaster.

He steps in front of Van, and Van is gone, forgotten.

There is only Jesper.

There has only ever been Jesper.

He is the moon covering the sun, drowning the world in darkness so that only he can shine, an eclipse at the end of the world.

"I'm sorry—" Angelina starts.

He puts a finger to her lips.

"Never be sorry. I listened to your song."

"I hope it's OK..."

She trails off, uncertain.

"It's a gift," he tells her. "Sometimes I feel like a lonely beast calling across a starlit valley, and finally, someone answered."

"I saw the valley. I saw the stars."

Jesper smiles and takes her face in both hands and kisses her forehead. "Come with me."

He twines their fingers and leads her away from the fire. She looks back over her shoulder and sees piles of white cloth on the glimmering sand, naked bodies twirling and dancing and grasping and writhing, sweat-slicked and sliding and slipping to the ground. Van watches her go, but Angelina can't see her face in the shadows, can't tell what she's thinking. She was glad to kiss Van, she thinks. She's always wanted to kiss a girl but has never quite known how.

Still, she'd rather be with Jesper.

Maybe he wants to—

No. Surely not.

She's just a whatever she is, and he's a god.

They are in the forest again, and she's barefoot now, and she trips, and then Jesper is carrying her. How is he so strong? Her arms go around his neck, and she breathes in the sublime perfume of his throat and wants to lick it but holds herself back. His fingers splay over her ribs, grasp the curve between hip and knee, grazing that tender area behind her thigh. She feels every place they intersect, tries to memorize this moment like a princess saved by a handsome prince, but her mind is muddy and thick, and she can't help wondering why everyone else gets to stay. Why she has to leave, has to be carried away like a child put away after bedtime. So long, farewell, auf wiedersehen, goodbye.

They do not go to her tiny house. Jesper carries her to the villa, past the fierce unicorn and up the stairs and into a room she has never seen before. Her heart quickens—his bedroom? There is indeed a bed hanging from chains, a king-sized swing mounded with pillows and furs. He places her there as reverently as a newborn in a cradle and covers her up with something delightfully soft. A lamb? Or just its skin?

"Sleep well, little starlit beast," he whispers, trailing fingers over her cheek.

"Where are you going? Why can't I stay?" she asks, the barest whisper.

"Soon," he promises. "Soon."

Inspiration, transformation
Bread to body and water to wine
Stay the same and die inside
Take the knife and draw the line

"CATERPILLAR OF SALT," TRACK #3 ON BLACK IDYLL,
WHAT'S THE STIGMATA?, KAKOPHONY RECORDS, 2020.

10

Angelina wakes up on the love seat in her tiny house, a little after noon. She is scrunched up to fit, her face pressed into the fabric. She does not know how she got here. She doesn't remember anything after drinking the wine. She can already tell that she is going to have the hangover of her life, despite the fact that she only had a few gulps of whatever was in the bottle buried in the sand.

Her mouth tastes like a coffin, and she rinses with water and looks out her window, toward the forest, trying to remember. Memories claw at her mind with ineffective little kitten paws. Maria was dancing. Van kissed her. And then Jesper carried her through the forest. That's all she has. Three shadowy flashes like a flicker of fish fins in dark water.

And what can she do about it? Nothing. She can't ask Van; that would just make things weird. She's too starstruck to speak to Maria Perez. And if Jesper really had to carry her away from the party like a naughty child, then she doesn't want to give him reason to remember it.

After a long, hot shower, she puts on a white dress and steps outside to another beautiful SoCal day. She only now realizes that she doesn't even know which tiny house belongs to Van; thus far, Van has always found her first, and she hasn't shown the appreciation and curiosity that a real friend would. She heads to the Well and finds a scattering of people quietly eating, each looking as hungover as a college freshman — vaguely green and greasy-skinned with bags under their eyes. It's almost a relief, that these beautiful people can look anything less than perfect. Angelina toasts a bagel, adds Beatrice's golden butter, grabs some green tea, and sits with the few people she knows.

"Where's Van?" she asks Thierry.

He shrugs Frenchly. "Haven't seen her. Just woke up. Feel like a horse kicked me in the head."

"That's drum night." Kierra's head is in her hands. "I love drum night, but I hate the morning after drum night."

Jorge groans. "Stop saying drum night."

"Which tiny house is hers?"

Thierry closes his eyes. "The one right beside yours. With polar bears. How do you not know this?"

Angelina feels like an idiot and resents it. "She just always found me first."

"She does that. I have never been that extroverted in my life." Kierra nibbles at her toast. "If you build a place for strange artists, I guess you have to understand that many of us are introverted, reclusive, or straight-up hermits."

Without Van around and with everyone looking like they have the flu, lunch is a bit of a bummer, so Angelina takes the rest of her bagel to go. As she passes the garden and sees white hats bobbing within, she wonders who found the dead chicken, and what they did with it, and how they felt about it. No one has mentioned it, but then again, it's not like they have a daily newspaper. Curiosity gets the best of her, and she approaches the nearest gardener.

"Do you need something?" Marnie asks with a polite smile. The hem of her skirt is stained brown, as are her bare feet. She does not look hungover, but she doesn't look happy, either.

"I saw something weird in the garden the other day," Angelina begins.

"Oh? Why were you in the garden?"

Her manner is so politely hostile that Angelina reflexively looks around for witnesses, but they are alone, standing by the vine-swaddled arbor. Marnie is holding a trowel—a sharp, black trowel.

"I thought everything was open to everyone. I'm sorry if that was intruding. I was actually going to ask if I could help out—"

"We have it under control, but thanks for checking in. Namaste." Marnie clasps her hands around the trowel and gives the little bow that Angelina has become accustomed to instead of the word "goodbye."

As Angelina walks away, she sees two white hats tilted together and supposes Marnie is telling Lisbon what has just occurred. It does not escape Angelina that Marnie ignored her attempt to get answers, but that she also didn't seem surprised, which means she probably knows perfectly well about the dead chicken. But is she covering it up? Or was she involved?

Marnie does not look like the kind of girl who ritualistically beheads chickens. She looks like an Olsen twin.

Angelina is entirely off-kilter now. She passes by her own house and goes to knock on Van's door, but it's propped open with a bucket. A woman she hasn't seen before is scrubbing the fridge, wearing a white canvas jumpsuit and long yellow gloves. She turns around when Angelina knocks.

"Is Van here?" she asks.

"No idea. I just get the units ready for new occupants." The woman is older but still beautiful in a sharp, hardened way. "So if this was her place, she must've gone back home."

"Do you know why?"

Because that doesn't make any sense to Angelina. Van seemed happy here and gave no indication that she wanted to leave.

Or maybe—

Did she get sent away for something that happened last night? For giving Angelina the wine, or kissing her? Or something that happened after that, when Angelina was already gone?

"Again, no idea. They pay me to clean and be discreet, so that's what I do." The woman turns back to the fridge, and Angelina glances around the small house.

It's quite similar to hers—identical, in fact. If Van made any changes to the décor, they've already been removed. Two big black garbage bags sit over by the stairs to the second floor, and Angelina can just see a white skirt spilling out, which suggests that wherever Van went, she didn't take her clothes.

But, well, again, all-white doesn't make sense anywhere else in the world. If she left, she would probably go back to dressing like normal people.

Angelina sits at the tiny table in her own tiny home, wondering what the hell is going on. Van was her source of information, and now Van is missing, and she doesn't know who else to ask. It seems very strange, but...

People in their twenties come and go all the time. Back at the coffee shop, they would receive a hundred résumés for an open position, go through all the trouble of selecting and interviewing and hiring a candidate, and then that person who had fought so hard for the job might never even show up, or show up once and then ghost. In college, kids would drop out mid-semester. In every part of life, people ebb and flow for reasons of their own. Angelina can't imagine why anyone would want to leave this place, but maybe Van's mom needed help, or maybe she had to go to a doctor, or maybe she was so embarrassed of kissing Angelina that she decided to flee the country. It's not Angelina's business, and if it was, Van would've left a note.

Satisfied with her reasoning, Angelina opens up her laptop and starts working on her next song. Last night, for all its confusion, has left her with several crystal-clear memories stamped in her mind. Starlight, fire, white bodies in movement, dancing and bowing like cranes. She is giddy as she types, the melody already forming, twisting, doubling back. She can still remember what it smelled like last night, when her lips were an inch away from Jesper's throat. Clean sweat, sandalwood, metal, ozone, and something astringent like green tea. If only she'd been in full control of her faculties so that she could've properly enjoyed it—and remembered more of it.

Her guitar feels solid in her hands, familiar and friendly. She doesn't stop playing and singing, not until there's a noise loud enough to break through her very expensive noise-canceling headphones. She blinks until she can see the world coalesce and is surprised to find Solomon standing in her open door. She thought she'd locked it, but it seems that she loses track of reality when she's writing here.

"Didn't mean to startle you," he says, eyes twinkling. He's wearing a white tank top tucked into crisp white linen pants. Silver chains hang in the black hair on his chest, and Angelina notices a brand on his upper arm but can't quite make it out. "Do you have a moment?"

"Sure."

One syllable to contain the enormity of what it means to be in the same room with someone who possesses this kind of charisma and power. His presence doesn't short-circuit her brain the way Jesper's does, but it's close. Solomon is not a large man, but he seems to fill the little house. He sits on her love seat, arms spread across the backrest, one leg crossed.

"How are you settling in?"

It's funny, she thinks, how what passes for small talk among normal people feels like a final exam in the presence of a celebrity.

"Well enough. It's a lot to take in."

He smirks. "It should be quite easy. A life of leisure. A relief from the everyday pains of the outside world. Don't you think?" His eyebrows raise in challenge.

Yup, it's a test.

"In many ways, yes." She picks her words carefully. "I worked as a secretary on campus, back at college. One of the lower-level administrators had this pink pen she loved. It had a little feather bauble on top. One day it went missing, and she sent a red-flagged email to the entire School of Social Work, including the dean, demanding that her pen be returned. I realized then that whatever environment you were in was like a snow globe. No matter what was happening outside in the real world—wars, disasters, tragedies—your world is limited to the snow globe that contains you. And in that little world, a pink pen can become the beginning of World War Three. So I'm learning to adjust to a new snow globe."

Solomon nods slowly, cocks his head. "And do you like your snow globe? Some people, they hate the snow."

Angelina looks around the little house.

The *free* little house humming with *free* electricity, dripping *free* water, full of *free* art supplies. "I can adapt to anything. And I'm working on my second song. But, hey. Do you know what happened to Van?"

"Van?"

"She lived next door. I saw her last night at the drum circle, but today a lady was cleaning out her house."

Solomon looks to the right as if he can see through walls.

The houses don't have windows on the sides; it's more private. "Oh, yes. She had an opportunity back in New York. A mural. Very high profile; very secret. I'm sure she'll be back when she's completed it."

"But her house is being given to someone else?"

A careless shrug. "If we have an empty house for a couple of months, that's one more person we can help. An empty house helps no one. People leave as they please. Freedom is part of the gift." He leans forward now, fingers steepled together. "Listen, love. How would you like an opportunity of your own?"

Angelina's fingers trace over the top of her laptop. "I'm already here, where everything is free. What more can there be?"

He smiles like Santa, or perhaps Willy Wonka. "We'd like to invite you to be more involved in House of Idyll. Would you like that?"

An impulsive twitch flows through Angelina's muscles, a full body yes. But she doesn't want to appear that eager. Eagerness is rarely attractive to people accustomed to power. "I'd definitely like to hear more."

"We have an inner circle. A sort of think tank, if you will. Come up to the villa this evening at seven and check it out. If it's not a good fit, you're still welcome here. We anticipate great things from you."

Angelina wants to grin so badly that her jaw aches, but she manages to keep it together. She knows the Inner Circle; the special people who eat with the band. "Sounds good. Do I need to bring anything? Is there a dress code?"

Solomon stands. "It's not a potluck, love. Just bring yourself. And wear the usual: all white. Ta." He does the namaste bow and strolls out her door. Everywhere the man goes, he looks like he's swanning about a horse track.

But!

Angelina got invited to—

The Inner Circle? The table of special people? And it's actually a think tank?

It doesn't matter.

Being near Solomon—and Nico—especially Jesper—it's a rush unlike anything she's ever known before. Just being around them pours art and passion into her soul, makes her fingers twitch to write. The music is all but gushing out of her. She was worried that she'd messed up somehow last night, but...

An invitation to the villa.

She stands and heads up to the Well. She has to look her best.

She has to look like one of them.

Feed me your secrets
Tell me no lies
Make of your heart
The ultimate prize
Wash yourself clean
Whiter than snow
I am the stag, you are the doe

"DIE DIE DIANA," TRACK #8 ON BLACK IDYLL,
RaWaR, KAKOPHONY RECORDS, 2018.

11

The walk to the villa feels different. Special. Like when debutantes used to line up to wait their turn and meet the queen and gain her favor. And like those debutantes, Angelina has chosen a long white dress. Her hair is down and brushed out smooth, with little braids pinned back. She's done gold makeup around her eyes and heavy mascara, and she's wearing gladiator sandals. She feels like a goddess.

OK, goddess in training, perhaps.

Trembling, slightly panicky, curious-but-terrified goddess in training.

She wonders if her neighbors know where she's going, where she's been especially invited to go. She doesn't want people to be jealous of her, doesn't want to be disliked, but she is thrilled to be stepping into the golden glow. There are upwards of fifty people around the property, probably, but the Inner Circle are the most special ones, the ones everyone watches. She has seen them traveling together like a pack of gleaming white wolves, leaning in to whisper at lunch, throwing back their heads to laugh like they live life in a movie montage. She never sat with the popular kids at school, but she'll accept the invite now.

She hasn't been inside the villa since her interview on that first day—

Or has she?

She has memories of the hallway, and a room with a giant swing?

Maybe that was just a dream.

In any case, she walks into the foyer and finds lit candles leading up the stairs, casting a warm, orange glow over the curving white walls and gleaming honey wood. Finding no one, she follows the firelit trail to a room she hasn't seen before. The villa is huge—at least a dozen rooms, plus tons of extra doors—but this seems like perhaps they knocked down a wall between two bedrooms. The ceilings are tall, every surface is white, and one entire wall is composed of glass, making the sky seem like it's the real wall.

"Shoes off, love," Solomon says from beside the door, as if he's been waiting for her. He's wearing a long white tunic, like a kurta, over white pants. His hair is down, and a silver necklace shines at his throat, a pendant nestled just under his collar. He winks at her and takes a seat.

Angelina now wishes she hadn't worn such complicated shoes. She unties the strings on her gladiator sandals and unwinds them from her X-impressed ankles as everyone in the room stares at her curiously, making her feel like an absolute fool. There's Solomon, Nico, and Manny sitting in a row of mod leather chairs. Maria Perez lounges on a white chaise. And then, draped over one of those enormous U-shaped couches, perhaps ten other people Angelina has seen around but never met, including the singer, actress, and chef, people she would consider celebrities—or maybe pre-celebrities. They, too, wear silver necklaces. She hasn't seen much jewelry here—there's none at all in Outfitting. All the men are wearing the same white kurta, which is not available at the store, and all the women are wearing a dress quite similar to the one Angelina has chosen but more... not exactly formal. Crisp? Her sundress feels like a little girl's flimsy costume compared to their sophisticated linen gowns. She wishes she had pockets, or a hoodie, or some way to hide. Their stares press into her skin, like she's just stepped into a spotlight.

Jesper appears in an arched doorway wearing a white kurta, but with nearly invisible white embroidery along the collar, sleeves, and hems; as always, he's just a little extra. His hair is pulled back in a ponytail, and he smiles as soon as he sees Angelina standing there.

"We're so glad you could join us." He does the namaste bow, and after an awkward pause, she returns it. "Welcome to the Inner Circle."

"Thanks—I'm glad to be here."

She has no idea what to do. They are all watching her expectantly with a strange eagerness, a... hunger?

"Please, take a seat." Jesper indicates one of two high-backed chairs. They are placed, to Angelina's dismay, in front of the room, with all the other seating arrayed to face them.

"What's happening here?" she asks, her voice low. "Solomon said it was like a think tank?"

"Just sit, and I'll explain."

Her choices are to sit or to leave, and so she sits.

The moment she is in the chair, it feels like everyone else sighs and the room relaxes. Jesper sits in the chair opposite hers. He's so beautiful that it makes her feel... bewitched? It's distracting. Just being around him is intoxicating.

"You know that the House of Idyll is an experiment in art and beauty," Jesper says, and she nods. "Perhaps you've heard it's lonely at the top. Most celebrities—" He looks down and chuckles. "I hate that word. But most celebrities are vapid and empty, chasing increasing risks and depravities. We don't want to become that way. We want to be around people who enrich us, who inspire us and make us feel more alive. So we choose the people we allow to get close to us. Solomon told you this was a think tank, and it is, a little. We run the business of the House of Idyll, decide who to invite and how to move forward. And we also create art together and simply enjoy the beauty of friendship." He smiles with all his dimples. "I know it may sound cheesy, but let's just say that money has a way of showing you who your true friends are. Do you understand?"

God, she does not feel worthy of this.

Who is she? No one.

"I think so," she says, aware of every muscle in her face, unsure where to look.

"But part of the process of inviting someone in is that we want to get to know them better. There are no lies in the

White Room. We offer one another the gift of total honesty and authenticity. What you're about to go through—it's like a trust fall. But for your soul." He reaches out and takes her hands from where they're laced in her lap. "Do you trust me, Angelina?"

"I— of course."

She looks around the room.

Jesper Idyll sings words that make her feel known, but she doesn't know these other people. She wishes it were just her and him, just the two of them.

He looks into her eyes, and she snaps into place like a puzzle piece.

"Have you always felt alone?" he asks.

Just like from the song.

"Yes," she murmurs.

She can't look away. She can barely blink. The world becomes a tunnel of light containing only two people. Everyone else fades away.

"Why?"

Her mouth falls open.

This is a very big question.

She doesn't want to bore him or embarrass herself, but...

He wants the truth.

He said so.

But...

"Why have you?" she asks.

Jesper's eyes twinkle. "A fair question. I was raised by a single mother, a nurse. She had to work a lot. I was an only child and spent most of my time home alone. We didn't have much money. I was never a— a guy's guy. I liked music and reading and just staring off into space. I liked having long hair and painting my nails black. I got bullied a lot. I would've done anything to just... be allowed to be myself. I couldn't even pretend to be like them. It just felt like a lie. I always doubted myself, thought maybe something was wrong with me. When I got into the performing arts high school and met Solomon, it got better. But that's why a lot of our early songs are about not fitting in. Because we didn't. And we were angry about it."

And yes, she knows most of this because she's been reading his interviews since she was fourteen and he was eighteen, but hearing it from him personally, seeing the tears in his eyes, the tightness in his mouth—it feels like a gift, that he will share this pain with her.

"My parents are Baptists," she says, matching his tone. "They were strict. Not very... huggy. I was always at church or Vacation Bible School. The only thing I was allowed to sing was hymns. They told me that Jesus loved the little children but hated who they became unless they were very specific people. I knew I liked boys, but I realized I liked girls, too, when I was in middle school. And I thought that meant I was going to hell. I did everything they wanted, and it was never enough." A rueful smile. "I didn't know who I was, but I knew there was something wrong with me, and it made me angry."

Jesper's fingers tighten around hers. "There's more, isn't there? I can feel it inside you, bubbling like lava. Let it out."

"They wanted me to date the preacher's son. I couldn't

stand him, but I wanted to make them happy. We went to homecoming. He took me out for spaghetti in his father's Mercedes. He was a perfect gentleman. But he insisted we leave homecoming early and drove me out to his dad's hunting cabin. I didn't want to go, but my parents wouldn't let me have a phone, and I couldn't stop him. I knew that if I made him mad, he would tell his dad, and then his dad would tell my parents. So I did what he told me to do."

A strangled sob escapes her. She has never told anyone this part, although she has tried to write about it many times and failed.

"I didn't know it was rape, at the time. He told me it was OK—that we were still virgins because we didn't... didn't do it the normal way. It hurt. And then I had to see him at church on Sunday. He told my dad we'd had a good night and he hoped to see me again. I made myself throw up on him so he'd stop asking me out. Fettuccini alfredo and garlic bread, lots of it. I still can't stand the smell of it, but I didn't know what to do except make myself disgusting. I've been on plenty of dates since then, and I've had a few one-night stands, but most men make me feel like an animal being hunted. So that's why I feel alone."

Jesper Idyll, still holding her hands, moves to his knees in front of her. He brings her hands to his lips and kisses them, then gazes into her eyes. It's like looking into the brightest blue sky of summer.

"You're not alone," he says fiercely. "And there is nothing wrong with you. You are perfect, exactly as you are. You are a unicorn among horses. You were never meant to fit in. It is better to be yourself, imperfectly, than to pretend to be anything else."

Jesper stands and pulls her with him. He turns her tenderly toward him, takes her jaw firmly but gently in his hands, and wipes away her tears with the flats of his callused thumbs.

"Angelina Yves, I find you worthy," he whispers, peering intently into her eyes. He reaches into his pocket and pulls out a silver necklace, which he fastens around her neck. The metal is still warm from his body when the pendant settles against her chest. He leans forward, his lips moving against the shell of her ear. "You're one of us now. I never want you to feel alone for a single moment." His hand finds hers again, and he squeezes it, and it feels like he's giving her his strength, his surety.

She squeezes back. "Thank you, Jesper."

And—

Wow.

She feels… like a new woman. Like she's a foot taller. Like she's clean and new and strong.

Like maybe she deserves to be here.

Jesper hugs her, and then Solomon is there to hug her, then Nico and Manny. Everyone in the room comes up to her, takes her hands, tells her she's brave and beautiful and that she did not deserve what happened to her and that they are glad she is here now. She has never felt so welcome anywhere, so loved. Even in church, where the whole point was to feel accepted, she always felt completely removed, but this, this belonging, being absorbed into this room full of beautiful artists…

It's like she's finally found where she belongs.

Someone puts a coupe in her hand, and then everyone is drinking champagne. Angelina's entire world is white and fire and bubbles and laughter. She feels drained, like she's run a damn mile, so she plops onto the couch and finds it to be the most comfortable thing she's ever sat on. She's talking to Maria Perez and an actress, and she's talking about the album, her album. She feels like they are friends, like they have always been friends. She is loose and lithe and limber and full of love for everyone. She is fiddling with her new pendant but has not yet discovered what it is, only that she imagines the metal still carries heat and atoms from Jesper's body, adding them to her own compilation and forging them together forever. Everyone else wears a unicorn pendant. She hopes hers is the same.

After the champagne, Manny—always the most responsible one in the band—reminds everyone that despite the feeling of celebration, they still have business to attend to. It's entirely mundane, so mundane that Angelina has trouble not throwing her head back to laugh as they pass around the menu for the Well next week and argue over whether it should be salmon croquettes or tuna tataki. They are considering offering an open spot to a young actor who got kicked off *Saturday Night Live*, but Maria argues that she knows an impoverished dancer who recently broke her ankle who would benefit more. They all agree they should schedule a class on lymphatic drainage and that it is absolutely essential to add snail mucin to the Idyllic facial care regimen.

They treat Angelina like she is one of them now. She learns

new names, is invited to sit with them at lunch; it's like *Mean Girls* except everyone is wearing white and no one is mean. Maria compliments her hair and says Angelina's voice reminds her of honey. Philip is a music producer, and he asks for her Instagram; if she's as good as Jesper says, he can get her some jobs as a backup vocalist. Manny tells her that he'll have a linen gown delivered to her tiny home before their next meeting.

Angelina does not know what she has done to earn her place here, but she will ride this high as long as she can.

She forgets to ask about Van.

She forgets to ask about anything.

When she has danced back to her tiny home and traded her dress for a white nightgown, she lifts the pendant from its chain. It *is* a unicorn.

Just like her.

You can't take this
You can't break this
Make it real, make me feel, no fake bliss
Darkened souls can't do white magic
Empty hearts make art that's tragic

"LEGERDEMAIN," TRACK #4 ON BLACK IDYLL.
(RE)HEARSE. KAKOPHONY RECORDS. 2014.

12

Weeks pass, and Angelina has never been happier and more productive. She's writing a new song every few days, which feels like a triumph. As she sings the harmonies, plays her new guitar, and mixes the sound, she loves what she hears. When she pulls up one of her old Instagram Reels, she is actively repulsed. How did these vapid, regurgitated love songs ever come from her mind? It is so obvious that she wasn't in love, that she wasn't even laboring under a real crush. She was pantomiming courtship with someone who didn't exist, and now that she has a real, actual crush, she can tell the difference. As the Black Idyll song goes, empty hearts make art that's tragic.

She goes to yoga, crochets a horrible granny square at Craft Night, learns tai chi, makes s'mores by the lake, sits in the front row at her first Empowerment Seminar and feels more hopeful and invigorated than she ever dreamed possible.

Her heart was empty, but now... now it's filling.

Like a dry reservoir after rain.

Life is coming back.

And maybe, just maybe, she's utterly infatuated with Jesper Idyll.

She sees him more frequently now, is growing accustomed to his nearness. Almost like exposure therapy, but instead of being terrified of spiders, she trembles in anticipation whenever he's around, her skin twitching like horseflesh.

With Van gone, Solomon suggests Angelina might take up the role of Welcome Wagon. At first, she is repelled; she is not an extrovert, and she honestly wasn't a big fan of the way Van just let herself in and out of her little home, even if it was to leave gifts. But then Jesper asks her about it in the lunch line, and his eyes are soft and kind like a stag in the forest, so she says yes. She's not sure she's capable of saying no to him. Fortunately, he hasn't asked anything so far that she wasn't more than willing to give.

She's on a text chain now with the Inner Circle—she literally has Jesper's cell number—and that is how she is assigned her first visitation. She reluctantly closes her MacBook, reapplies her lip gloss, brushes her hair, adjusts her pendant, and heads out to earn her keep. Before this, they haven't required her to do a single thing other than pursue her happiness. It's the least she can do.

Of course the new recruit is right next door, at what was once Van's house. When she knocks, she expects to find Maria's broken ballerina friend or the young actor, the two possibilities they'd argued about. Instead, it is a woman—almost a girl. She seems terribly young, thin and elegant and shaky as a greyhound, which tracks, because her eyes carry the cagey distrust of a kicked dog. A battered backpack sits on the ground, and Angelina notes that the girl's hoodie and jeans are filthy and worn.

"Can I help you?" the girl asks.

Angelina's heart crumples for this poor, beautiful creature. Someone hurt her, that much is clear.

"Jesper and Solomon asked me to stop by and help you get settled," she says with her friendliest and most genuine smile. "I'm pretty new, too. I know it feels really weird, at first."

"Jesper asked you to stop by?" The girl's perfect jaw drops. "*The* Jesper Idyll?"

From her shock, Angelina can only assume that the girl didn't have the same audience she did in the all-white room. Interesting. She thought all new members went through a similar procedure.

"The very one. Have you met him yet?"

The girl's eyes are huge. "No. I'm kind of scared to. He's like, THE Jesper Idyll, you know? Is he as hot in person?"

Angelina chuckles. "He's everything you want him to be. So can I show you around? We can fill up your fridge, get some lunch, hit Outfitting?"

The girl nods. "Yeah. OK. If it's all free. Solomon said it was free. It is, right? But like, how is that possible?"

Speaking softly, Angelina explains everything. The girl— her name is Megan—has trouble believing this is real, but she is eager for food and quickly embraces the concept of free clothes. When she leaves the dressing room in a white long-sleeved tee, there are bruises visible at her throat, her wrists; in the brighter light, there's a fading dark smear around one eye. She's a runaway, found by Solomon and Mr. B walking along the highway. Not an artist, not a singer, not a writer—barely educated. Angelina understood that people were brought here to create art, and she wonders if maybe Megan is only a pity case.

"What do you plan to do with your time here?" she asks as they walk back to Megan's house with a basket full of apples and peanut butter and crackers.

"Solomon said they could use me in videos. Like, modeling and stuff."

Angelina can see why. Megan has the alien, lanky, carved-out beauty she's only ever seen in magazines. "Well, I'm right next door if you have any questions. I think you'll like it here."

Megan bites into an apple, juice running down her chin and throat like a teen Eve. "Yeah, me, too."

Back in her house, Angelina wants to ask the Inner Circle about Megan—what's actually happening here? Did they take in a teen runaway or adopt the next Heidi Klum? Is there a therapist on staff—someone to help guide Megan to healing? She's only seventeen. So young. Does she need a parent's permission to be in the compound? Or are her parents the ones who hurt her? Something about her is just so dreadfully broken.

Angelina types and retypes the text fifty times before giving up.

Maybe it's not true, but it feels like saying the wrong thing could get her kicked out, even if it's in defense of an innocent young soul. She doesn't want to insult anyone, doesn't want to assume they haven't already taken precautions to keep Megan safe.

It comes down to this: Does she trust Jesper and Solomon? She has to.

And besides, she's right next door and home working most of the day. She'll keep an eye out on her neighbor, make sure everyone is being just as kind and respectful as the girl deserves. No one here has given her any cause for concern, and she's fairly certain that creeping on a teen girl would get someone thrown out. Nico was once all over the news for putting a guy in a stranglehold for threatening a woman in downtown New York, and Black Idyll have always been advocates for various charities benefiting women's rights.

Still, as she types, she listens. Cracks her door open. And when Megan leaves sometime in the afternoon to walk toward the villa, Angelina watches from her porch, wondering whether the girl was invited or is going there for her own reasons.

She's jumpy for the rest of the day, and she wonders if this is how Van felt, like she was responsible for the health and welfare of each new recruit. She goes to dinner early and is pleased to find Megan there, chatting with Ji and Kierra. Angelina waves to them before joining the Inner Circle at their usual table.

"How's Megan settling in?" Solomon asks.

"Pretty well. She had a lot of questions, and I hope I gave her the right answers. I'm kind of worried about her, actually. She's just so young..." She trails off.

Solomon cocks his head. "She is young. I'm glad we could offer her a safe place to make better choices. And I'm glad you're nearby in case she needs something more."

"I saw her walking up to the villa today..." She trails off again, painfully aware that she's not actually asking the questions she wants to ask.

Solomon's lips twitch; he is also aware. "Yes, once we were able to contact her parents and finish some paperwork, we needed her to sign a few more things. It's complicated when someone is underage, but I couldn't leave her where I found her."

"And her parents just let her go?"

His eyes go dark as his jaw clenches. "After a bit of pressure, yes. We have vicious lawyers on retainer and no patience for abusers. We took care of everything."

Angelina wants to ask how—how do you force parents who are clearly neglectful or abusive to give up their rights? Was there a threat—a lawsuit? Or did money exchange hands? She looks to where Megan is laughing with Ji and Kierra and wonders if it really matters, so long as this poor girl can finally experience comfort and safety.

"Are you ready for tonight?" Maria asks with her gorgeous accent, leaning in like they're girlfriends.

"What's tonight?"

Maria raises sharp eyebrows. "It is the full moon. And you know what that means."

No.

No, Angelina does not know that.

But asking would only serve to highlight that she's not completely part of the in-group, so she just smiles and says, "Of course."

After lunch, she considers the Inner Circle and who might be the best one to ask about this full moon business. They all seem equally and impossibly out of reach, beautiful or powerful or famous or, quite often, all three. Angelina feels like a child when she's around them, like things are happening somewhere over her head, important things that don't make sense, that filter down to her like whispers at a cocktail party. She would feel like a fool confessing to any of these gorgeous specimens that she doesn't know what's happening, even when they assume she does.

She gives the namaste bow and goes home to attack the internet, looking for any hints about Black Idyll or the House of Idyll and the full moon. The only connection she finds is the song "Harvest Moon", which has always been one of her favorites, but which she doubts is connected. That single was from their first album, and the video was all in shades of black and white with blood that looked like ink. It ended in this insane sort of blood rave in an all-white room. Angelina remembers an interview where Nico said the "blood" was actually just chocolate syrup and that the shoot made him very hungry and also messed up his hair.

As the sun sets, she paces. All the Instagram posts lauding the benefits of tiny homes never mention that they are very bad for pacing. Still, she doesn't want to go outside; something special is going to happen; she can feel it. There is an excitement, a gravitas in the air. She needs to stay inside and wait for it to happen. Driven half mad by the tension, she finally puts on her new white linen dress and brushes out her hair, just in case whatever occurs is on the more formal side.

It's dark now, and still nothing. No texts, no knock on her door. She stands on her upstairs balcony as the wind ruffles her long dress, feeling like a widow waiting for a sea captain who's already died, listening for the sound of drums at the waterside or music at the villa or other evidence of more perfect people having a wonderful time without her.

Finally she gives up and goes to bed, still in her linen gown.

"Fuck you, Maria," she mutters to herself.

What a terrible thing, to get someone's hopes up.

She sleeps poorly, always waiting for her door to squeak—

And then it does.

Her eyes jolt open in the darkness as steady steps creak toward the stairs. Angelina fluffs her hair over her pillow prettily and lies on her back, pulling her dress down where it's all bunched up from her tossing and turning. If she's to play Lucy Westenra, then Dracula will find her looking beautiful.

The feet on her stairs are measured and, she thinks, bare. There is a formality, a weight to each step. In the scant light that filters in from the damnable curtain, she sees a female shape clad in a long white dress. Goddammit, she should've stayed awake, guzzled coffee and been more mindful of wrinkling her own dress. Delicate fingers stroke her shoulder all the way down to her hand, where they entwine with her own and tug. Feeling like an absolute idiot, she sits up. She can't tell who the woman is; she's wearing a strange mask, all white with barely the suggestion of features. At the second tug of her fingers, she stands. There is not much room here on the second story of a tiny home, but the other woman turns and walks down the stairs. Angelina has no choice but to follow.

Outside on the porch, the woman slips on a pair of sandals and cocks her head in a way that suggests Angelina should do the same. Once she has obeyed, the woman leads her into the dark. She is holding a candle in an old-fashioned candleholder. There is a solemnity to this experience, to the woman's bride-like pacing, that suggests Angelina should remain silent and refrain from questioning what's happening.

She expects the woman to lead her toward the lake or the villa, but she instead walks out past the stables and the Well and is absorbed by a looming wall of whispering black leaves. This is a different part of the forest, one Angelina has not yet explored or even really given much thought. This was, she assumed, the property's border. There is a narrow path, humble and rough, lacking the playful sculptures and hanging birds. Ahead of her, the woman moves like a ghost, her white dress a pale bloom against the darkness, glowing in the light of the full moon. Branches pluck at Angelina's dress, tug at her hair. Her heart quickens; it's happening, the thing she was waiting for, but she still doesn't know what it is or what's expected of her.

Light filters through the shadows, strange flickers of color luring her close like a crooked finger. She'd expected a fire, the lick of red and the scent of smoke, but oddly, this is not fire; the glow is an unnatural purple. The path opens onto a clearing, an impossibly circular space cut from the thicker forest. Instead of dirt and roots and sticks, there is a carpet of thick green grass, and Angelina doesn't require urging or instruction to slip her feet out of her sandals and curl her toes into the luxurious pelt of it. Strangely, there is almost perfect and complete silence. The only noise is the brush of fabric, the crunch of soles on grass, an occasional animalistic grunt.

All around the clearing, figures move to a beat Angelina can't hear. Their lithe bodies shine as bright as lighthouses, their dresses and pants and shirts of bright bluish-white topped with matching identical masks that completely hide their faces. They wear heavy black headphones, their arms up and holding, oddly, glow sticks, their wrists and necks encircled by the same. This is the least environmentally friendly thing she's seen since arriving, and yet there's something almost... holy... about it. Thanks to a few well-placed black lights, everyone and everything has an otherworldly glow that leaves trails in the inky darkness.

A figure detaches from—

Really?

A DJ stand. Turntables and a chunky laptop. The DJ appears to be male and is wearing the same white mask. He walks over to Angelina, and even in the darkness, even disguised, she knows that it's Solomon; she would recognize that lanky, louche, slouching stride anywhere. Her guide has disappeared into the throng and could be any of the willowy girls in white undulating through the night like jellyfish in the deepest part of the sea.

Solomon is in front of her now, blocking her view. His long fingers hold out a small pill.

"This is MDMA," he whispers in her ear, his breath warm against her temple. "Have you done it before?"

The breath catches in her throat.

"No."

"This is a choice, so listen carefully. MDMA is a chemical that increases dopamine, serotonin, and norepinephrine. It heightens trust and openness and reduces anxiety and fear. They call it ecstasy for this reason. It does not cause harm if it has been properly formulated, which I assure you this has. If you'd like to stay at this event, you will take this pill. If you don't wish to participate, you'll be guided home. There are no negative repercussions for choosing to go home, and if you decide to stay, nothing will happen without your spoken consent. There will always be a sober person keeping watch. Do you understand?"

Angelina's entire world shrinks to the size of a very small pill that she can't quite see. She has never done drugs, has never had any particular interest in them, and yet... when will she encounter a safer environment in which to experiment? She is with people she trusts who possess the resources to handle any problem. There is no life-or-death job demanding a cup of pee, no sharp-eyed boss waiting to catch her hungover. And she is quite certain that if anyone can obtain high quality drugs, it's the wealthiest band in the world.

If she leaves, she will experience a sweeping regret.

Shame. Embarrassment.

She will be the lonely girl who finally got the invite to the cool kids' party and said no.

But if she stays...

She opens her mouth, and the rock star in the mask places the pill on her tongue with all the reverence of a pope's benediction.

Look above and look below
What you reap is what you sow
There are no answers in the sky
The rain does not care if you're dry
Give in, give up, give me your heart
I promise I won't tear it apart
Moon, moon, harvest moon
Make you crazy as a loon
Moon, moon, harvest moon
He will come, he'll call you soon

"HARVEST MOON," TRACK #7 ON BLACK IDYLL,
(RE)HEARSE, KAKOPHONY RECORDS, 2014.

13

The he pill is bitter. Angelina doesn't know if she's supposed to swallow or chew, so she lets it dissolve as she waits for further instructions. She can't see Solomon's face behind the glowing mask, but she knows he's smiling, pleased with her. He puts big headphones over her ears, and the music, previously just the gentlest faraway suggestion, fills her entire soul. She wants to ask when the pill will kick in, how long it will last, if it's as addictive as her health teacher promised back in eighth grade. But Solomon is already gone, back at the DJ stand, one hand in the air, pointing at the stars. A masked dancer slings a necklace of glow sticks over Angelina's head, and everything else is pulsating with the music, but she's holding still, waiting for—it—to start, whatever *it* is. The dancers feel something she doesn't; she is still just as uncertain and inhibited as ever. She feels so strangely outside the party.

And then she feels it—

A presence at her back, big and solid. A man, standing so

close that the heat of his body radiates deliciously. Her muscles go rigid as a mask is placed over her face; with the headphones on and the music thumping, she can't hear anything happening in the outside world and she feels like she's just stepped into a snare. Her vision narrows to tunnels, her breath warm against the plastic. Firm hands tighten the elastic, briefly run gentle fingers through her hair, smoothing it down to the small of her back.

He moves around to face her, and even though she already knew it was Jesper, now she knows it bone-deep. His eyes are a flash of electric lightning blue behind his mask, his pale hair under the headphones long and flowing, almost lavender under the black lights, his bare chest white as marble and so spare and muscular that his ribs remind her of a fish's gills. A flat belly and those marvelous V marks plunge into low-slung white leather jeans that fit him like a second skin. She wishes she could see his back, see the unicorn tattoo she knows is there. He leans in and holds an earpiece away from her head to ask, "Will you dance with me?"

Angelina wants to ask him if he took the same pill, if it's kicked in yet, if he's just asking her to be polite, like in the Black Idyll video for "Chic to Geek" when the football player asked out the quiet goth girl because he felt sorry for her, and she reticently, shyly, naively agreed before drinking his blood on their fake date, turning him into a hot goth guy. Except—

Jesper wrote that song, directed that video.

He hates pity.

She nods her consent, and his fingers catch her hips. EDM

pumps into her ears, pounds through her body, fills her like a cup. It feels silly, at first, swaying along to music that only exists in her ears, but she soon remembers that everyone else is having the same experience, so even if she feels separate, really, she's just at a different kind of rave — not that she's ever been to a rave. Her forehead begins to sweat behind the mask, her body warming at the closeness of Jesper's rippling abs, his hips pressed against her as his hand finds the small of her back, trapping her, sending her heart twitching like a rabbit.

The song subtly changes, and it's another one by Black Idyll, she realizes, turned into a symphony of bass and layers, a lotus of unfolding petals. She closes her eyes to savor the perfection of the sound, and her skin grows thin and tremulous and opens like a door. Jesper's fingers press eloquently against her back, the spread velvet antler tips of a glorious stag. It's a delicious pressure, and she moves into him, desperate for his closeness, wondering if perhaps they will merge like wet clay now that her skin has ceased to act as a barrier. Their atoms are mixing, their essences entwining like smoke. They began on the edge of the circle, but now they're somehow in the middle of it all, the center of the universe, a new sun being born from glittering vapor.

Her fingers have been captured, and someone else pulls her close — a woman. Maria. Angelina recognizes her long, dark hair, her dancer's grace, the lively flicker of the black eyes behind her mask. One of her dress straps has fallen, revealing one perfect breast, and she's so beautiful that Angelina wants to cry with joy. Jesper is behind her now, pressing against her, and Maria puts her wrists around Angelina's neck, and they are dancing, the three of them, more vapor swirling together, the beginning of a galaxy newly sparkling.

Angelina has never felt so open, so perfect, so loved, so glorious, so included. She has always looked in at parties as if from behind a window, wondering how other people know exactly what to do and say, how they can start dancing when no one else is dancing or call the first song on a karaoke machine. Now she understands. She was always part of the party; the window never existed. She trapped herself behind fear. Anyone can begin the dance; anyone can sing. The first person offers the gift of permission to all. The party did not push her away; she pushed the party away.

This thought happens as quickly as fingers snapping, and then she is transfixed by the softness of Maria's hair, her fingers plunged into the rippling rivers of satiny ink. They are moving, bouncing, jumping, but she longs to touch Maria's cheek, run fingers along the sharpness of her collarbones, to know her as a cartographer knows a map.

Maria suddenly twirls away, pulled by a planet with more gravity, and then a new man is there. When everyone wears the same mask and nearly the same clothes, when everyone is so perfect and they are all part of the same whole, it becomes difficult to identify one person. It's like sun-warm taffy, she thinks, all stuck together until it's no longer individual pieces, just one sweet, gooey mass.

But this—

This is Nico.

She knows his hair, and she knows his tattoos. Although the inside of her closet was secretly dominated by images of Jesper when she was younger, there was one poster with all four band members wearing only kilts and boots. Much about them has changed in ten years, but Nico's tattoos have not. Greek myths dance up his arms, all in the same blackline illustrative style. Medusa, the Minotaur, Poseidon, Actaeon. He holds out a hand, an offering. She looks back over her shoulder at Jesper, and he nods as if giving permission. She does not want to leave Jesper, but she does not want to refuse Nico. They are all one, after all. It would be the same as refusing herself.

Her fingers reach out, twine with Nico's fingers, big and rough from years of drumming. They are like two vines curling in tandem, and she is overjoyed to realize that Jesper is still with her, his hands firm on her hips, almost possessive. She is caught between the two men, their bodies moving with hers, following hers, and she relishes the coiled energy barely contained by Nico's skin. His hips grind with her, and warmth pools in her belly, her body desperate to touch along every possible surface.

A thought burbles up from somewhere:

She is in the middle of a Black Idyll sandwich.

This is her teenage dream come true.

These two—they were always her favorites.

Laughter fills her like jingle bells, happiness shining like a sunbeam.

This, here now, this is all she's ever wanted.

For once in her life, she's exactly where she's always wanted to be, where she's meant to be. It's like she generally either lives in the future, worrying, or in the past, fretting—but right here, right this moment, she is in the glorious now, and nothing could ever possibly be wrong in the world.

The song changes to one she doesn't know, and the bodies blissfully joined to hers melt away. Every song and snippet of song so far has been from Black Idyll, every voice in her head one she knows by heart, even if sped up or slowed down or pitched differently. This new music is dark and slow, a dragon's heartbeat echoing down a dark cavern. Hands clasp her own hands, and she is pulled into a circle. Girl, boy, girl, boy, she notices. All of the black lights turn off except one. Shadows move in the periphery, and someone drapes something over her head and shoulders—a cloak. It is soft as gossamer and dark as pitch, and she feels like a wizard as she softly sways in place and enjoys the liquid swirl of the fabric.

Now everyone in the circle is the same: A black cloak with a white mask.

Angelina looks around and sees herself multiplied eleven times.

This is curious, she thinks, but she wants to move, to feel, to touch.

Her hands are caught, but it's not enough to satisfy her needs.

Something special is happening; her needs are not currently the focus. She is one with this circle, and the circle bids her wait, and so she will wait, even as she is certain that if she is not touched, she will burst like a piñata at any moment.

The music continues to thump in her ears, slow and steady,

voices chanting in a language she doesn't know. And still, even with the headphones on, she senses it—

Something moving in the forest.

She looks past the circle and sees the most beautiful thing in the entire world.

A unicorn.

Massive. Pure snow white with enormous, shaggy feet and cloven hooves. A gleaming, wavy mane flows down past its neck, its forelock falling slightly over one intelligent eye. And the horn—

God, it really has a horn, not some made up prop!

A real horn, twisted and black.

No one else seems to see it. They are all focused on the circle. Angelina looks from side to side, but no one else acknowledges her excitement, her wonder. She lets go of the hands holding hers and backs out of the circle, walking behind the cloaked figures as they stand there like statues cast of obsidian.

"Is nobody seeing this?" she says.

With her headphones on, she can't even hear her own voice. Of course no one else can hear her.

She waves a hand in front of the masked figure beside her. She can no longer tell who is who. There is no hair, no tattoos, even their feet are now covered by the gossamer robes. There is no response to her waving, nor to her breaking the circle. The hands of the people beside her clutch air, as if she is still there, among them. As if she has not left the circle.

Just on the edge of the forest, the unicorn stamps a foot and snorts. He is waiting, Angelina realizes. Waiting for her.

She has no experience with horses, but this unicorn is no horse. He is something different, something special and beautiful and magical. She reaches out to stroke the velvet gray of his nose. His breath is hot on her hands, his lips soft as they brush over her fingers, taking in her scent. He could bite her hand off if he wished, but instead, he does the strangest thing.

He lies down.

First his front legs, then his back. Then he is on his belly, his massive neck majestically curved. When Angelina doesn't move, he tosses his head toward his back.

He... wants her to ride.

This is another invitation, she thinks.

Everything here demands consent.

She does not have to accept this offer...

But she will.

Hitching up her cloak and dress, she sits astride the unicorn's broad back, feeling absolutely ridiculous until he stands. As he pitches forward, she wraps her arms around his neck, and then she is sitting five feet off the ground, her bare feet dangling from the unicorn's warm, white sides. Her fingers tangle in his mane, and he steps carefully into the forest, following a path only he can see.

The unicorn is hot beneath her, his every exhalation palpable between her thighs. His fur is a gloriously soft canvas, and her fingers release his mane to brush along his neck, his shoulders, his back. She feels safe and cradled, as if the unicorn is taking care of her, just as Solomon did earlier. The black light is long gone, but the full moon casts a wan smile over their promenade.

Angelina is surprised when the unicorn emerges from the forest and walks eagerly toward a small building she has never seen before. It looks older than most things on the property, built of adobe but small and humble—an old church. The door is open, a spill of warm light welcoming her inside.

The unicorn stops, its hide quivering under Angelina's sweat-slick thighs, urging her to slide off onto the ground. Once there, she runs a hand along the hard muscles of his neck, but he throws his head, impatient.

"Do I go inside?" Angelina asks.

The unicorn gives one nod, almost a bow.

"I don't want to leave you."

He nudges her with his nose, gentle but insistent.

And, well, who is Angelina to argue with a unicorn?

With one last pat, she walks toward the open door. Inside, candles drip from windowsills and ledges and shine from an old candelabra. The church is small, just six old pews. She looks back to the unicorn, but he is gone.

She steps within, the stone floor cold under her feet. But— no. There is a carpet of flower petals. Red roses, leading her forward. It feels like something is unfolding for her, something special and precious. Her headphones continue to thump with the music, the chanting, the bass that matches her heart. She dabs a finger into a pool of warm wax, desperate for sensation.

And then he is there, in the doorway.

A man in a black cloak and mask, but not the plain white mask.

A unicorn mask.

Like everything at House of Idyll, it is a work of sublime art, flawlessly expressed. If she didn't know better, if she hadn't recently touched the actual nose of an actual unicorn, she would think someone had cut off a horse's head and hollowed it out and—

No.

That's so weird. So grim.

This is a piece of art crafted by an artist, an artist who has also seen the real unicorn.

The man steps through the door, his cloak billowing behind him. He stands before Angelina, tall and still.

"Welcome, Angelina."

The voice comes to her through the headphones, soft against the background of thumping and chanting.

And that's when she knows that this is all part of the show, the experience, the full moon excitement Maria intimated earlier today. This must be her initiation to the Inner Circle. She is giddy now, thrilled to be part of the—it—she was so eager to discover. She is one of them, she is special, she is in the circle, they are all one, her skin needs so badly to be touched, she is an open door and someone, someone must step through.

"Will you give yourself to me?" the voice asks.

She does not answer immediately, and the man in the unicorn mask steps close, his chest to hers, his need pressed against her belly through the silky robe.

The voice is one she knows by heart.

It belongs to Jesper Idyll.

"Yes," she whispers. "I will."

Poor little girl, all alone in the dark
He doesn't know her bite is worse than
    his bark
She thinks it's pity, he thinks she's
    pretty
Soon his neck will wear her mark
Chic to geek, cool to freak
High school's pretty fucking bleak,
    oh yeah

"CHIC TO GEEK," TRACK #2 ON BLACK IDYLL,
NEVER RHYME FRIEND WITH END. KAKOPHONY RECORDS, 2016.

14

Angelina wakes up in her own bed with the worst headache of her fucking life. She is completely naked, and there is no sign of her white dress from last night. She immediately closes her eyes and drags probing fingers through her memories. They are surprisingly available, playing back through her mind like a sitcom she's watched a thousand times.

When she gave her consent, Jesper began to undress her, teasing her with his fingers because he couldn't kiss her. He did not remove the mask. There was something strange and exotic about that, no mouths, only eyes and fingers by candlelight. When she tried to touch him, he pulled away and shook his head. God, she'd wanted to feel every crevice of that body, smell and taste the skin she'd lusted after for so long. She wanted to know the contours of his ribs, claim the secret places behind his ears and knees, feel the ridges and curves of him. But he denied her that sensation she so craved and distracted her with touches of his own.

He splayed her over a pew, played her like a violin, drove her to a crescendo. When she writhed and begged him to take her, he bent her over a velvet-draped table and took her from behind, a bestial thrust that might have been savage if she hadn't been so ready and wanting. He was big; she remembers that with an exquisite ache that continues this morning. She had never come that hard before in her entire life. Multiple times. Until he did, and then he withdrew.

The troubling part: she can't remember if he was wearing protection.

She's fairly certain he wasn't.

Thank God she has an IUD; both for her heavy, painful periods and because even if she sucks at relationships, she still had needs that one-night stands were happy to fulfill. She long ago decided she wouldn't let one asshole ruin her relationship with sex. But—Jesus, she barebacked it with a rock star. Who knows how many people he's been with? She'll have to ask later today if he's been tested recently.

This is not a question she ever thought she would have reason to ask Jesper Idyll.

How embarrassing.

But then again—

After last night, will things change between them?

Was it a peculiar initiation, a ritual, or does Jesper see her, really see her?

Will it—

Could it happen again?

Or is it some sort of Inner Circle prima nocta, a claiming

he performs with every new recruit? Is that why he wore the mask? To symbolize that in that moment, he wasn't Jesper the man but Jesper the...

The leader. The king. This is his world, his playground.

She assumes he is accustomed to getting what he wants.

Yes, he required consent, but who could say no to that voice, that face, that body, that soul?

The longer she lies in bed, the more restless she becomes. She is coated in sweat. Her mouth tastes like something died in it. Her jaw hurts. And she's fairly certain she didn't pee after last night's festivities, which is not ideal for the female biome.

In the shower, she argues with herself. Was last night a triumph or an embarrassment? Is she an accepted member of the Inner Circle who had the privilege of sleeping with her high school crush, enjoying her first multiple orgasms under his talented fingertips? Or is she an idiot teenybopper who gave herself to a near-stranger, body and soul, exposing herself to all sorts of diseases and possibly the gossip of everyone here—and in a church, no less?

And there's another question rapping against her aching skull like a woodpecker:

Why does she remember all of that in exquisite detail and yet have absolutely no idea how she got back to her own home? Once he had finished, he withdrew. He laid a hand against her back, fingers spread and claiming. And then he was gone. She stood and turned, hoping perhaps Jesper would take off the mask and say something to break the ice, something funny and private and sweet. But all she saw was a bone-white figure walking out the door, the mask still in place. He did not take his cloak.

Most troubling of all, she now remembers one very important detail.

Jesper Idyll's back features a tattoo of a rampant unicorn. Angelina would know it anywhere. She has studied it intensely via posters and gossip websites. But the figure walking out of the church and into the night?

He had no such tattoo.

So who was it, in the mask?

Not Jesper. It couldn't be. Unless he's had the tattoo removed? But she doubts it. She's fairly certain she's seen the horn poking up when he wore a tank top one day. It obviously wasn't Solomon. Nico is tan with tattoos and more muscular than the mystery man. And Manny has tanned skin with thick black hair on his arms and legs, while the man in the church was pale—plus, Manny is gay. So it wasn't anyone from Black Idyll.

She thinks back to all the men from the Inner Circle, but none of them match the body type and height she recalls from last night. Except Jesper. It had to be Jesper. That was his voice, but—

Well, anyone's voice can come through headphones, can't it?

No. It *was* Jesper. It's almost embarrassing how well she has memorized the shape of his body. Maybe he put makeup over his tattoo for the ritual. Or maybe she's misremembering. She was, she well knows, drugged.

MDMA. Ecstasy.

Pure, or so Solomon says.

After her shower, she gets online to research more about this drug she knows nothing about but accepted into her body with an almost idiotic innocence. What she reads confirms what she remembers from the experience, how she was in her right mind and aware of everything but far more open, connected, experimental, and sexual than usual. It also explains how she feels today—profoundly shitty. Almost depressed. Definitely paranoid. Like she's felt the sun's warmth but is now firmly planted under a dark cloud.

It sucks.

Nobody told her about this part.

How being so close to something beautiful only reminds you how alone you truly are when it's gone.

She next does a search for Jesper Idyll's tattoos and is rewarded with reassurance that she has remembered the unicorn on his back with absolute clarity. An image from just a few weeks ago of Jesper walking in a fashion show confirms that the unicorn is still there, pawing the air furiously. This knowledge only makes Angelina feel more uncertain.

Whose bare dick was inside her last night?

She stares at the Inner Circle chat, reading everyone's thoughts on last night's Moon Rave, as they call it.

"Best rave ever!"

"Sol, that set was fire!!"

Lots of hearts, lots of heart eyes, lots of fire.

A few mentions of today's various aches and pangs, and a

reminder that the Well has extra electrolytes, tea, and anti-inflammatories on offer today.

Angelina's skin is twitching like the unicorn's did last night—

Not the guy in the mask, but the actual, literal unicorn.

A trained horse?

It must've been.

This compound is so huge that there are plenty of places for stables, even if she's never seen them. Or maybe they carted him in like a birthday pony. Maybe that's what he's used for—they strap on the horn and walk him around in circles with little kids on his back, and he's been trained to do the lying down thing. But how did he know to take her to the church? And where is it?

Angelina gets dressed in white jeans and a tank, needing more armor than usual to face the world. She heads for the Well and finds furoshiki-wrapped boxes in a neat stack by the bagels with a label reading, *For those needing a little extra self-care today ;).* She takes one, plus an Idyllic Electrolyte Water and a box of sushi. No one is around, but it's that weird time between lunch and dinner when the House of Idyll undergoes its own version of a siesta.

When she's done eating her sushi and drinking an elderflower-flavored health beverage that promises to raise her vibrations and heal her heart with various mushrooms and adaptogens plus hand-harvested salt and carbon-neutral honey, she contemplates her next step. Before she asks questions that might bite her in the ass, she needs to confirm what she saw last night.

It's easy enough to find the path that led her to the rave now that she knows where to look. Recently cut, it's as wide as a golf cart, which explains how Solomon could have an entire DJ stand in the middle of the forest. Last night, it felt like she was following a ghost through endless darkness, but today she is following tire treads.

The clearing looks almost garish in the daylight. The soft grass she remembers is actually squares of sod. A few sad glow-sticks rest among the plush green, their magic dead and dull under the California sun. She finds the indentations left from the DJ stand and a few discarded masks—and a few discarded condoms. The cleanup crew in their crisp white uniforms has not yet arrived, apparently, but knowing what she knows of House of Idyll, this place will again be pristine and sea turtle friendly by end of day.

As she walks the periphery, she searches for the other path, the one the unicorn followed as she sat astride its powerful back. This trail was not harshly cut, and the only prints she sees are the imprints of large cloven hooves. Which... horses do not have. Horse hooves are U-shaped. So maybe the "unicorn" was wearing special horseshoes or something?

It's not long before she finds the church. It is exactly as she remembers it.

On the outside, at least. On the inside, there are the pews, the melted candles, the velvet-covered table.

And on the carpet of rose petals lies Megan in a long white dress, covered in blood.

Sometimes it's just too much
A child can die from lack of touch
And me, I'm just a child
Trapped in this skeleton, tender and mild
Release would be so sweet
Turn myself from pain to meat
I'm broken so broken I'm choking
   and stoking the fire inside
I cannot abide

"KISS KISS KMS," TRACK #3 ON BLACK IDYLL.
(RE)HEARSE, KAKOPHONY RECORDS, 2014.

15

Angelina immediately understands that Megan is dead.

She sees the blood, so much blood, spread out in sticky angel wings, pooling on the stone, wicking into the white dress in shades of pink. She sees Megan's open eyes, the fly perched on the tips of long, mascara-coated lashes. She sees the wounds on each elegant wrist, the razor blade gleaming dully on the girl's pale palm.

And still Angelina runs toward her, shakes her bony shoulder, calls her name. She knows there will be no answer, but she has to try. She is an animal now, a creature of instinct, a series of impulses, a desperate wish to see Megan blink and laugh and sit up, saying it was all part of the initiation.

How long is she on her knees in the blood, begging the girl to wake up?

Animals don't measure time.

Long enough. She is there long enough.

Her knees are slick and sticky, and it wakes her up to reality.

She stands and fumbles for her phone, wipes her blood-wet hands off on her jeans. 9-1-1 are three numbers that she's had memorized since she was a toddler, and yet her fingers are shaking so hard that she has difficulty making the call.

"Megan killed herself," she tells the soft-voiced woman who answers. "Please. Please help."

The operator asks for her address, and she doesn't know it.

"House of Idyll," she says. "A church in the forest. They brought me—I don't know. I don't know where we are. There's a lake. A forest."

She can hear the nice woman talking to someone else. A new voice comes on the line. A man. He is firm and certain.

"You're at House of Idyll, is that correct?" he asks.

"Yes. Please help. She's— please—"

"We'll take care of it."

And then he hangs up.

But 9-1-1 isn't supposed to hang up, are they?

They're supposed to stay on the line and ask questions and offer comfort.

Her phone rings, and she stares at it in wonder for several seconds before remembering how to answer it.

"Hello?"

"Angelina, it's Jesper. Are you OK?"

A strangled laugh escapes her. "No. No. Very much no."

"Where are you?"

"The church from last night. In the forest."

"I'm on my way."

She looks down. Her white jeans have become the canvas

for a Jackson Pollock of gore. The coagulating liquid has soaked into the fibers, spreading in shapes that are almost beautiful, like watercolors. She looks at the—

No.

She looks at the table.

It looks exactly the same as it did last night, the velvet cover askew. She can still see the imprint of her torso, the indents where she clutched the blanket in tense fingers as she cried out, her eyes closed, her entire world shrunk down to the feeling of skin against skin, wet against wet, muscle and bone and a need so great she nearly broke in two. By that time, she'd shed her linen dress like an ill-fitting skin, leaving it by the door, and—

No.

It's not—

It's—

Megan is wearing it.

She's wearing Angelina's dress.

Angelina's Inner Circle dress of crisp white linen is soaked in blood.

But why would Megan do this? Why would she come here? Why would she put on this dress? Why? Why?

Angelina saw the girl's wrists when she arrived, and she can see them now. Megan's flesh is no stranger to the blade. Hash marks make ladders up and down her arms, and Angelina is certain that if she could see her legs, they would wear their own tattoos, a secret language, each mark representing some small release of chosen pain. Megan was troubled, but coming here...

This place should've been the end to her troubles.

A land of safety and plenty.

Why would she hurt herself?

Why could she possibly want to die?

A shadow in the doorway blocks the light.

Jesper.

He hurries to Angelina, sinks to his knees, draws her into his chest, wraps his arms around her. His voice—like an angel—crooning in her ear. Telling her it will be alright. Telling her not to look.

"Why?" she asks him. "Why?"

"She had a hard life." His voice is soft as he presses her head against his chest. "Domestic violence at home. Sex trafficking after she ran away. Some people don't know how to live when they're not in panic mode. Some people are simply too broken. We wanted so much more for her."

Angelina rubs at her eyes and immediately realizes she is rubbing blood into her own tears. She is covered in it—her hands, her clothes, her hair. If Jesper has noticed, he doesn't seem to care. His heart thumps doggedly under her reddened palm.

Once she stops shaking, he helps her to stand and steadies her with a hand on each shoulder. His eyes, so warm and vulnerable, gaze into her own, and she feels seen, every inch of her seen and cared for. He kisses her forehead, lays his cheek against the crown of her head.

"I'm so sorry you had to see this, Angelina."

"I'm sorry she— she—"

"I know. I know. I am, too."

"Mr. Idyll?"

162

Jesper looks up, but he does not release Angelina or step away. There's a policeman at the door, peeking in. Solomon puts a hand on the officer's arm and slides inside first.

"Angelina, let's get you back home," he says.

"I'll take her." Jesper looks down at her. "Are you ready? We should get you cleaned up." When she nods, he guides her out the door. She looks back at the single officer entering the room, Solomon's voice a quiet burble. Shouldn't there be more police? An ambulance? Firefighters? Something more than a white golf cart with the Black Idyll logo on the hood?

Jesper laces his fingers through hers and guides her through the forest. She can't see the path, but he can. Time passes strangely, her eyes focusing and unfocusing. She sees a long, white hair caught in a tree's bark and pulls it free, rubbing the wiry tail hair between bloodied fingertips.

Instead of heading to her tiny home, Jesper takes her to the villa. Just inside, he kneels to remove her shoes, then his own. He leads her upstairs to an enormous bedroom she's never seen and walks her directly to a massive shower with multiple heads and teak benches. When the water is hot enough to steam the mirror, he asks her if she'll be OK on her own. She nods, and he gives her privacy to undress. The water is glorious; she's forgotten what it feels like to stand in a shower big enough that she can turn around without bumping a hip. She washes her hair and scrubs her skin. When Jesper returns, she is sitting on the floor, her knees under her chin. All the pink water has swirled away down the drain, the white tile washed clean. Angelina wishes she could feel that unsullied.

Jesper turns off the water and drapes her in a fluffy white robe. He's showered, too, and changed into white pajamas, his feet bare.

"I brought you a pile of clothes," he says. "Didn't know what you'd prefer."

Soon she is curled up in matching pajamas in an enormous bed, surrounded by mounds of crisp pillows, drinking hot chocolate with Jesper Idyll. He has a projector and a big white wall, and he offers her a laptop so she can choose something to watch. Normally, she would be hyper-fixated on selecting something that would impress him or make her seem cool, but she just puts on her favorite comfort movie and settles in.

"I love this one," he says. "Wait. We need popcorn."

And then, as if he is a perfectly normal person, Jesper gallops from the room and returns with a bowl of slightly burnt microwave popcorn that Angelina does not eat. Sometime during the movie, she falls asleep, and when she wakes, Jesper is setting up a sushi dinner at a low table surrounded by flat cushions.

Jesper Idyll is... serving her.

It's so bizarre she could laugh. But she doesn't. She wonders if she will ever laugh again.

She has no appetite, and the food has no flavor. She stuffs a few bites down, aware that Jesper is watching her like a teacup that's about to fall off a table.

"If you're willing, we're having a meeting of the Inner Circle tonight," he says softly. "We find that coming together and talking through our feelings helps when... when these things happen."

Angelina blinks at him. "Do these things happen often?"

He shakes his head vehemently. "No. We had a trail runner get bitten by a rattlesnake, and he didn't have signal and died before we could find him. And one other suicide, a long time ago. The mind of an artist... it can be a dark place."

She knows he is remembering their fifth band member, Vivian, and she knows he refuses to talk about that, at least in the public eye.

He looks down ruefully. "Did you know I had an attempt? When I was young. Just sixteen. When our first record company dropped us. It sounds so stupid, saying it now, but I thought the world was over."

He turns over one wrist, takes her fingers and runs them over a tattoo of a moth. She can't see the scar under the black ink, but she can feel it. Vertical, just like Megan's. But healed.

That—that finally gets her attention.

Angelina has read everything that has ever been said about Jesper Idyll, but this was not in the gossip rags. "They said you went to rehab..."

"But not for drugs or alcohol. For depression. I needed medication and therapy. It's what started my journey to House of Idyll. I wanted to give troubled artists a safe space, the resources they needed. Hell, if we could provide universal basic income, we would. There's so much art that wants to be made."

"Knock, knock." Solomon stands in the doorway; he looks like a sad and noble lion. "We're ready if you are."

Jesper offers Angelina his hand. It means something more, now that she knows what's under the black and white moths on each wrist. She briefly wonders if she should wear something nicer, but—well, Jesper is in pajamas, too.

Solomon continues on, but Jesper pulls her close, one hand on her back, and tucks a stray lock of hair behind her ear. His eyes are so soft, welcome and warm as a summer pool. Up close, she can see little freckles she's never noticed before, the tiniest laugh lines at the corners of his eyes. He's more real, close up.

"I need you to understand something," he says, voice low.

"OK..."

"What happens in the Inner Circle is special. These are people I trust with my life, with my secrets. The band especially—I've been with these guys through thick and thin for fifteen years. And the others have been carefully chosen. Tested. But I need you to know that... you're becoming special, too." He looks down at her lips. "Can I kiss you?"

She almost laughs, this is so insane, but she can sense a new shyness about him. He actually thinks there's a chance she'll say no.

"What about Maria?"

His eyes slide away. "She left last night. We argued. She saw how I look at you. Caught me listening to your song. She was more into me than I was into her, to be honest. That happens to me a lot. I feel like people don't see me. The real me. They just see Jesper Idyll. They think I'm the person in the videos. They want more than I am. It gets tiring." He searches her face as he cups her jaw. "Do you? Do you see me?"

Angelina is too raw to be anything but honest. "I want to. I'm looking. I'm calling across the starlit valley."

His face lights up. "I hear that call. I hear it in your song. You make me want to sit in the dark with my guitar and discover things." He looks down, ducks his head like a little boy offering flowers. "You never answered..."

Angelina's body is tingling like she's made of champagne. He smells of vanilla and white flowers and wildness, his hair glinting like strings of gold.

"Yes?"

She doesn't mean for it to be a question, but she is questioning everything.

Jesper's eyes crinkle up, his hands cupping her face tenderly as his lips land on hers. So soft, so gentle. He rests his forehead against hers briefly and murmurs, "Thank you."

Emboldened, she hugs him, arms wrapping around his back as she lays her head against his chest. "You don't need to ask. I'll speak up if something isn't working for me. You don't seem like a stranger to body language."

"I've always been an advanced reader." He tips her chin up and kisses her again, his tongue barely dancing along the seal of her lips. "Now come on. They're waiting for us. This is going to be intense, but... well, just remember that it's me, OK?"

He doesn't release her hand, but her hackles go up as they walk down the hall.

What is going to be intense? And why?

The Inner Circle has convened in the room with the squashy couches, but everyone is somber and quiet. There are, again, two chairs in front. Jesper leads Angelina to one, and he takes the other. Is he... going to therapize her? Again? In front of everyone?

When he speaks, his voice is more formal—the voice he uses in interviews. "Angelina, you've been through a lot today. And last night. We know you have a lot of questions, and this is a safe space to work through things. We've all taken a step into the unknown, and we've all suffered tragedies. Usually not in the same twenty-four hours." His smile is sad and rueful. "Last time you sat here, I asked you questions. This time, you can ask me questions. You can ask me anything."

Her throat is dry, her lips suddenly chapped. She has questions, but they have an audience. If only this were private, just her and Jesper. Why didn't she ask him anything, that whole time they were together in his room? It's like she's just now waking up from shock.

"Why didn't an ambulance come for Megan?" she begins.

"Because she was beyond saving." Jesper's eyes are wet, and he suddenly looks quite young. "We have to protect this place and the people in it, so we handle things quietly. If there had been any chance of saving her, we would've done everything in our power to help. Helicopters, whatever it took."

But...

"How did you know she was beyond saving? I found her. I made the call. And I was alone."

Jesper leans in. He bites his lip. His eyes look everywhere except directly at her; whatever he's about to say, he doesn't want to say it. "Because there are cameras everywhere here. There have to be. We immediately checked the footage. It's for insurance purposes. It's not monitored, and we only consult the logs if we need to."

Hot shame flushes her cheeks, and now she can't meet his eyes. "So what happened the night before—it's saved somewhere? And anyone could just—"

"No! No. Our system is the best in the world. Unhackable. When... when certain things happen, the footage is deleted. Immediately. Some things are just as damning to us as they are to the other people involved."

Understanding that she has been recorded without her knowledge—

Or maybe she signed her rights away in the contract. She must have.

She can almost remember it now. *A right to record.*

Shit.

Now she's upset, but she's also angry.

Angry enough to ask what she really wants to know.

"When was your last STI test?"

His lips twitch, a pained chuckle escaping his perfect lips. "The first of the month. I am very careful. And I had a vasectomy several years ago. No accidents."

"How many women have you taken to the church in the forest?"

There's something guarded about him now. He sits back, knees spread, hands clasped. "Me? *I* don't take anyone there."

"But—"

"Masks exist so we have something to hide behind. To become something new. They are tools of transformation.

What happens between two souls wearing masks is a magic of its own. Don't you think?"

Her body still aches from how hard he fucked her, but she does not say that out loud. She does not admit that it *felt* like magic, like they created their own world, like something glorious and powerful and entirely new was awakened and released from her soul as she dug her fingers into the velvet and screamed into the night.

"How many of these people has *the unicorn* claimed, then?"

Jesper's eyes are points of ice, drilling into her soul. "Only you, Angelina. Only you. No one else here has been chosen."

He is hunting
He is a hunter
Darling I can't be
Any blunter
And when he finds you
He will claim you
His velvet kisses
Will break and maim you
Mark you from within, make you
    one with him
When a good lay becomes prey
    the border dims

"RELEASE THE HOUNDS," TRACK #3 ON BLACK
IDYLL, RaWaR, KAKOPHONY RECORDS, 2018.

16

"What is she talking about?" a burgeoning actress named Jessica asks. "What church? What unicorn?" She looks around the room, arms crossed. "Seriously. Am I missing something?"

Solomon leans back, his arm tossed casually over the sofa's pillows. "Angelina had quite the experience at the rave last night," he says smoothly. "Your first time on ecstasy, I believe? She saw things. Hallucinations. Is that not correct?"

The look Solomon is giving her—hard, knowing.

"I definitely saw things. But I know what I saw."

Jessica throws herself back against the couch, pouting. "God, I wish it still made me feel that way. My tolerance sucks."

"Did you have any more questions for me? For us?" Jesper asks.

Angelina has a thousand questions. What was real last night? What wasn't? Was it Jesper she was with, or someone else? Who? Why was Megan wearing her dress? Why was

Megan there at all? Was she at the rave? And why the ever-loving-fuck are they throwing silent drug raves in the middle of the forest during the full moon?

Because rock stars, is all she can guess.

Because they can.

Because most people, if asked, "Would you like to go to a silent rave with amazing music under the full moon and shivering stars and take perfectly crafted ecstasy with no repercussions and dance with the most beautiful people in the world, including your teenage crush, while you feel connected to the universe in a way you never imagined in all your lonely days?"—most people would say yes without a second thought, just like Angelina did.

"What about Megan?" she asks. "What happens now?"

Jesper's head hangs. "It's out of our control. She was emancipated, but the coroner will contact her parents and let them decide." He looks down, his fingers flickering like he's playing guitar chords. "Should we do a memorial for her? I know she was only here for a few days, but she was still one of us."

Something in Angelina's heart relaxes. That feels right. A memorial. Megan was a troubled girl, and she deserves to be remembered.

"We should. I think that would help with—"

"Closure," Jesper finishes, matching her smile.

*

It happens two days later. Everyone is invited, and everyone attends. There is a wreath of white flowers with a black and white photo of Megan that Thierry must've taken right after she arrived. She's laughing in the Well, easy and smiling in all white. This photo could be on the cover of *Vogue*. The poor girl had such potential—and that was just her face. Angelina should've reached out more, should've gotten to know her better. She was asked to act as the Welcome Wagon, and she did, but maybe that's why this death is hitting her so hard. Not only did she find the body, but she feels like she should've done more, even in the few hours she had.

The four members of Black Idyll stand by the wreath. Nico has a hand drum, Manny has a white acoustic guitar, Solomon holds a white dove. Jesper is barefoot, and he sings "Gone Too Soon," which was used as a slow dance song at Angelina's senior prom even though it is clearly a sad song about saying goodbye to a dead person. His voice is crystal clear and perfect, absolutely heartbreaking. His eyes are closed as he sings, his hair back in a ponytail. There are people who would pay five figures to see Black Idyll perform like this, Angelina thinks, a private concert. She has only ever heard them in recordings. What a privilege that she gets to experience the raw beauty of Jesper's voice with Manny's harmony. As the last note draws out, Solomon releases the dove. It flutters up into the clear blue sky and disappears over the lake.

Life returns to whatever normal is now. Angelina works on her album, and she eats lunch and dinner at the Well with the Inner Circle, and she goes to Nico's next hot yoga class and lays her mat next to Jesper, and during Shivasana when she's supposed to be practicing death, his fingers catwalk across the sun-drenched wooden boards to find hers. The young actor who got kicked off *Saturday Night Live* arrives and is given the tiny home that belonged to Van and then Megan. Angelina welcomes him and shows him around and laughs at his jokes and wonders if he knows that the last occupant of his home is dead. When he asks her why they all wear white, she realizes that she no longer feels the need to wear anything else. White has become comfortable for her. Breezy. She loves tossing her clothes in the bin and picking out new ones. She loves her long dresses and the fact that she's given up on bras. She's seen Jesper look at her, seen his lips quirk up as he watches her move. She has never felt so beautiful, so strong, so free.

During the next drum circle, Jesper plucks a bottle of champagne from the sand and leads her back to the swinging bed in the big house and makes love to her with infinite care and slowness. She is tipsy and bubbly, but she is certain now that it was him in the unicorn mask; she knows this body, and she knows what it can do to her. She does not need ecstasy to be driven to raptures, doubled over the hanging bed, feeling Jesper's rough-tipped fingers untwining her very soul.

Weeks pass. Some nights she sleeps at home, some nights she sleeps over with Jesper. She likes the comfort of her own house, and she likes sharing his space, and he seems to appreciate that she isn't trying to strangle him with her affection. One morning she finds two dozen white roses dominating her kitchen table, along with a note from Jesper. The band has flown out to Madison Square Garden to perform at the Grammys and will be gone for four days. He is sorry to leave her but promises her a present when he returns.

At first she is — well, not jealous. She would've appreciated an offer to accompany them. But what was she going to do — sit around his hotel room while he practices and gets fitted for his costume? Stand around while he's in makeup, drinking green tea and being bored out of her mind? He's a rock star. He never made her any promises. And despite the many compliments he lavishes upon her and the decidedly dirty things he whispers to her, he has never said words like "love" or "exclusive" or "boyfriend." Whatever they have is unusual, and she has understood from the start that she does not own this man, that he would chafe against any kind of leash. But also that he does not own her. He isn't bound, and neither is she.

Not that she has her eye on anyone else in House of Idyll. Perhaps they are all beautiful to a one, but no one can compare to Jesper. No one ever could.

On the night of the Grammys, everyone gathers at the Well to watch Black Idyll's performance. They do "Love Song of the Moth" from their latest album, *The Succulent Reaping*, and everyone in the Well sings along as Jesper, Solomon, Manny, and Nico perform in sequin-spangled white velvet. They toast with prosecco and stick around to watch the band present an award they've already won to an up-and-coming band who look like middle schoolers by comparison. They hug the younger boys and clap for them, and then everyone loses interest and the Well clears out quickly. The sky is thick with clouds as Angelina returns to her little house and settles into bed, the air pregnant with energy and the wind heavy with the promise of thunder.

A noise wakes her: rain. Another fierce storm. Her head is only a few feet from the ceiling, after all. If Jesper were here, she would've asked to stay over in the villa, where there's a little more insulation from the fury of the tempest. But there's another sound fighting the pounding rain—a horse's whinny?

She pads downstairs and opens her front door. The small porch offers almost no protection from the slanting rain, and she shields her eyes with her hand. There are light shapes among the rain-black in the forest, uneasy masses shivering just behind the tree line.

Horses.

The same ones she saw across the lake.

She knows they are palomino and dun and gray, but they're ghastly and ghostly in the wan light, stark white when lightning flashes. They move nervously, throwing their heads and stamping their feet, rising up on their back hooves and tossing their manes. They stare at her and snort, their breath leaving little puffs of air in a night that's colder than South Cali has any right to be.

Soaked, her nightgown clinging to her skin, Angelina stares back at the horses, trying to understand what is happening. What do they want? Why are they here? Did they live in the barn once, before Black Idyll bought the ranch? Did they return here seeking safety when thunder began to shake the earth and the trees bent over almost double in the lashing wind? Should she go to them? What would she even do? How could she help?

No.

No, that's stupid. She's a soft, squishy human with very little horse experience, and she is not going to go outside in a violent squall just to get trampled by terrified wild things. For a long time, they regard each other. Lightning strikes, again and again, followed by the echo of thunder. The ground quivers under Angelina's feet. Something is happening, but she doesn't know what.

She sneezes, and the spell is broken. It's the middle of the night and she is staring at horses as if they are doing something of great cosmic importance instead of seeking shelter from a storm. She closes the door, strips out of her nightgown, and changes into a new one. Back in her bed after checking that the deadbolt is engaged—why? Why? Does she think the horses are trying to get in?—she lies on her back and stares up at the ceiling. A dark spot begins to form, so small that it could be mistaken for a shadow. But the shadow grows, radiating out like an amoeba doubling in size again and again, spreading and spreading and spreading, and then a single drop of water falls on her cheek. Another dark spot forms, and more raindrops plink onto her bed, staining the white sheets a darker gray.

"What the hell?" she mutters, scrambling out of bed.

This tiny house—it's practically new. Watertight. There's no way rain could get through that roof, even with a storm this aggressive. It makes no sense.

And then there's something else that makes even less sense:

The sound of a fist rapping against glass.

Someone is on her balcony.

She crawls to the sliding glass door and moves the curtains aside.

He's—

Something is—

There.

A form.

A darker shadow. Standing on the other side of the glass.

Like a man, but the head—

In growing horror, Angelina stands until she is face to face with a naked man wearing a unicorn mask. He puts a white hand to the glass, and she instantly notices that there is no tattoo on the wrist. No moth.

It cannot be Jesper Idyll.

Who the fuck is on her balcony?

Her eyes don't leave the mask as her fingers fumble for the lock, making sure it's engaged. His hand is flat against the wet pane, pale as a frog's belly, the fingers too long, and she backs away slowly, watching, watching.

He does not move. He makes no sound. Dirty rain courses down his grub-white body. His penis is erect and large, almost purple.

What the fuck? What the fuck?

She stumbles when the backs of her legs hit the bed, and that's when the panic sets in.

She turns and nearly falls down the steep, narrow steps. If she fell, if she hit her head—

No.

She can walk down steps. She doesn't have to run like this

is a horror movie. It's not like he's banging against the glass. It's not like he could break it with those stretching white fingers. It's not like he can get in.

Her foot slips on the last step and she nearly falls, and then she's on the ground floor. She opens drawer after drawer and finds nothing sharper than a spoon. When every meal is catered by professional chefs, no one needs a big-ass murder knife.

There are no weapons here—

Jesus, even her shoes are just flappy sandals.

What if he's climbing down from the balcony—

Wait, how did he get up there in the first place? How long was he there, watching her sleep through the filmy curtain?

She needs to call the police—

Her phone is upstairs, charging by her bed.

She can't go back up there.

Not now. She just heard the door slide open, the sound of the storm amplified as wet feet step deliberately onto the gray plank floor of her bedroom.

Fuck.

Angelina throws open the front door.

The horses are gone.

She runs.

Gone too soon, you're gone too soon
The sun is slaughtered by the moon
The autumn follows summer's swoon
You're gone too soon, gone too soon
I loved you then, I know you now
You're underground, torn by the plow
Your quiet broken by the dark woods'
   sough
My love, you're gone too soon

"GONE TOO SOON," TRACK #10 ON BLACK IDYLL,
THINGS GOT DARK, KAKOPHONY RECORDS, 2022.

The tiny houses squat like malevolent goblins, each darker and more forbidding than the next. No lights shine in their identical windows, no doors sit open. Angelina runs past them all and toward the one person who currently represents comfort. She doesn't know if Jesper is back from the Grammys, but the villa is big and sturdy and has many places to hide. If nothing else, she can grab some piece of sculpture off a shelf and throw it at the— the whatever he is.

As she runs, she glances behind to see if she's being followed, but there is no visibility. The night is ink-black, the rain falling sideways in sheets as sharp as a guillotine's blade. Her bare feet prickle with cold on the slick and muddy path. The villa suddenly appears, the porch lights always lit, the driftwood unicorn sculpture visible from the front window, steady as a security guard. She's almost to the front steps, and then she's scrambling up and into the foyer. The door opens easily, and she slams it behind her and throws the lock, putting her back against the old, heavy wood.

The change is so sudden that her ears ring. Warmth, quiet, stillness; the storm can't reach her here. Somewhere deeper inside, she hears the soft thump of music. Maybe the same music from the full moon rave. She regrets the dirt she's brought into this sanctuary, the brown puddles she leaves in her wake as she ventures further within.

"Jesper?" she calls. "Solomon?"

They are the ones she knows the best, but to be honest, she would take any friendly face now. Any person wearing clothes and not hiding behind some weird fucking mask. Any person without a rain-slick erection and freakishly long fingers.

No one answers her call, and in that moment, she realizes that for someone who has spent many, many hours in this massive home, she does not know the full layout. Is there a kitchen with knives? A landline phone? A panic room? How many doors might be sitting unlocked? She needs to find out. And lock them.

Room to room she passes like a ghost, gazing out each window, her heart a Kakophony, hoping she won't see a palm pressed against dark glass. When she finds the kitchen, she is pleased to see that it's decked out for someone who cares about cooking, which means the knives are exquisitely sharp. She's never held a Wüsthof before, but she might as well test out its legendary blade fighting off an attacker.

There—a back door. She locks it and continues on her quest. All along, her ears are twitching for the sound of wet feet on marble, her shoulders tense. What does he even want? And is he— the same guy who—

Fuck.

This is so messed up. She hasn't given this topic as much thought as it requires.

One night of pseudo-therapy with the Inner Circle is not enough to answer the question of who pretended to be Jesper Idyll to fuck her while she was high.

Satisfied now that all the doors to the outside are locked, she heads up the stairs, angling for Jesper's room. If the band isn't back yet, she will at least feel better behind that locked door. There's no phone, but—

Well, there are cameras, aren't there?

Cameras everywhere, she was told.

Not that it will do her much good if the guy in the unicorn mask wants to hurt her. It's not monitored. At least the expensive surveillance system will be great for piecing together her eventual murder for some award-winning true crime podcast.

On the top stair, thumping music slinks along the ground like mist. It's as brackish as a sleeping pulse, steady and slow and heavy and earthy, the perfect backdrop to the pounding rain. It's coming from a room she's never seen before. The door is closed, a seam of flickering light broken by shadows where it meets the floor.

"Hello?" she calls again. "Jesper?"

It's Jesper she wants. Jesper she needs. Jesper who will make everything better, just like he did when she was sixteen and felt like shattered glass.

She opens the door and...

What the fuck is happening?

In a world dominated by white, this place is as harsh and lurid as a wound. Dark red velvet drapes every wall. Turkish rugs cover the floors. Multiple video cameras are set up on tripods, and between them sit heavy iron candelabras that look like they were stolen from a crypt. The candles are black and red, dozens of them, dripping and pooling. Against the far wall is an enormous black wood X—the kind of thing she read about in that book about dime-store bondage that scandalized all the coffee moms as they secretly devoured it.

Hanging from the giant X is a woman—Maria?

Maria in a long white dress, her head hanging limp, her arms in manacles.

Around Maria's body three robed figures turn to face Angelina.

All three wear masks.

Not the blank white ones from the rave, but big, elaborate ones of white papier-mâché.

A stag, a rabbit, a unicorn.

That fucking unicorn.

Oh.

Oh, God.

"What the fuck?" Angelina murmurs, hands up like she could possibly fend off three men, even with the knife.

The unicorn mask flies off, and it's Jesper, his hair mussed, dark makeup smeared around his eyes, making his irises look white in the candlelight.

"Angelina, wait!" he says.

"No. No no no," she mutters.

"It's not what it looks like."

He steps toward her, and under his black robes, she is grateful to see his suit from the Grammys, blinding white.

At least he's not naked.

At least he's not standing in front of Maria's body with an erection.

But Maria—

Why? What have they done?

Angelina feels behind her for the open space to the hallway.

But someone pushes through, shutting the door.

Blocking it.

A man in an owl mask.

"We can't let you leave," he says.

X-rated, hexed, fated
Come to me soft, sweet, sedated
Let me lay you on the stone
Altar waiting, cold as bone
Come to me of your free will
Calm your heart, be silent, still
Give yourself up to my whims
Give yourself to me, to him
Let me make you scream and cry
From today until you die

"ALTER ALTAR," TRACK #9 ON BLACK IDYLL,
WHAT'S THE STIGMATA?. KAKOPHONY RECORDS. 2020.

18

And this is it: everything comes down to the light shining on the edge of a very expensive knife in Angelina's trembling hand. Whatever happened to Maria will not happen to her. Oh, hell no. She is a final girl. She will stab her way out of this fucking room or die trying. Her fingers tighten—

With a motion so quick she doesn't see it, the man in the owl mask shoves the knife aside, grabs her hand, and presses in a place that make her fingers jump, forcing her to drop it. She leaps back; a falling knife has no handle, her mother always said, and now is the wrong time to be barefoot in a killing room.

She squats to pick it up again, but a white loafer lands on the handle.

"Angelina, snap out of it," a familiar voice says gently.

Solomon.

She looks from Jesper to the stag, the rabbit, the owl, her eyes desperate and pleading for this to not be exactly what it looks like.

Solomon takes his mask off next, his locs up in a bun under the owl's high forehead.

"Well, love, looks like you've just fucked up our next music video. You don't get a producing credit for that, you know." His smile is wry, and he digs his thumb knuckle into the corner of his heavily lined eye like a tired child.

"What?" is all she can say.

The rabbit and stag masks are removed by their mysterious owners, revealing Manny and Nico. Manny looks annoyed as hell—he's the Type-A one, always frugal and ultra punctual—while Nico looks more concerned, with a little V between his green eyes.

"What's got you jumpy?" he asks. "Carrying a knife around? Wait. One of my Wüsthofs? Sol, get your foot off that!" Nico hurries over in his robe and grabs the knife, checking it for... for... whatever would ruin a billionaire's kitchen toy. "It's fine." He refocuses on Angelina. "You look like you've seen a ghost."

She can only shake her head and look at them, the masks, the big X, Maria's body.

"What did you do to her?" she asks.

Maria's head flies up, and she's grinning with those huge white veneers. "They said I could be in a video, so I did full hair and makeup, but they're just making me dangle here with hair over my face," she says with a laugh. "Silly boys and their toys. If we're taking a break, someone let me out. My hands are asleep."

Nico hurries to her, helps her down. She leans into him, her makeup flawless, and then exits the room like she's wearing a pageant gown instead of a filmy white negligee. "There's still Gatorade in the fridge, right?" she calls over her shoulder.

"Red and green," Manny says. "I went to Costco."

It's such a normal thing to say that Angelina's legs give out and she sits heavily, staring at what she can now see is clearly a video recording she has interrupted. There are lights perched in the corners, a table of gleaming surgical tools interspersed with musical instruments. Manny goes from camera to camera, pressing buttons, muttering. The robes even have the Black Idyll crest embroidered on the back.

"Jesus Christ," she mutters. "I'm sorry, but Jesus Christ."

Jesper winces. "I guess it does look a little sinister, if you just showed up."

The feeling returns to Angelina's extremities; she's shaking. "Why are you recording a fake satanic ritual at two in the morning? Don't you guys— I mean— wasn't your last video recorded by McG on a sound stage in Iceland?"

At that, Jesper chuckles and drops his robe to come sit beside her. His hand lands on her knee, and she flinches before resettling. He's being her goat, she realizes. He's steadying her, a human thundershirt. "Yes, it was, and it was way too cold, and we had some... personality clashes. We wanted to go old-school with this one. Get some black and white footage— almost found footage, like our first video—like 'Un1c0rn'. Very *Blair Witch*, you know? We got back from the Grammys, and the cross had finally been delivered and installed, and we were all hyped up, and we figured we'd give it a run-through and see how it looked on film."

"But... Maria said you made her do full hair and makeup?"

Jesper shakes his head, his beautiful hair glowing in the candlelight. "Maria chose to do full hair and makeup because she lives for that sort of thing. She's supposed to be playing a poor peasant girl. She's honestly overdone for the part." He looks Angelina up and down, his eyes alight. "Guys. Change of plan. What do you think?"

Nico and Solomon and Manny stop to look at her, considering. The touch of their regard is palpable, crawling from her head, down her wet nightgown, to her bare feet. She crosses her arms over her chest, quite certain that every part of her flesh is visible.

"Brilliant," Solomon says. "Innocent, raw beauty. Pallid, terrorized."

"That's not the compliment you think it is," she growls.

Jesper reaches for her hand. He's so incredibly warm, so real. His touch refills her like he's some kind of human phone charger. It's uncanny.

"Angelina, will you be in our next video? You're perfect for it. You're perfect in general."

The breath catches in her throat.

Black Idyll... wants her to be in a video?

"You'll be paid well, of course," Manny breaks in. "We'll need to get you into SAG. Or I guess it falls under Taft–Hartley. Anyway, we can give it a try and get into the paperwork tomorrow."

Jesper looks to Nico. "Will you go tell Maria?"

Nico grimaces, nods, and slips out of the room, taking his

knife with him. Angelina feels a brief sense of shame—like this is a form of girl-on-girl violence. Maria has been kind to her, and now she's stealing Maria's job?

"I thought you and Maria..." she trails off.

Jesper shrugs. "It is what it is. We parted on good terms and got to talking at the after-party. She's always welcome here. But I think—we think—you're perfect for this part. You have something she doesn't. This ethereal, spiritual quality."

She snorts. "I'm scared out of my mind. What you're seeing is vulnerability and terror. I probably look like a ghost."

His smile is sweet, tender, inspired. "Maybe a ghost is what we need." His eyes fly wide, and he gets that far-off look. "Maybe a ghost is what we need. The living aren't giving, they're full of greed. When you've already lost, when you're already gone. A queen can never be a pawn." He looks up at Solomon, who is diligently typing into his phone like he's accustomed to this sort of thing. Jesper brings Angelina's hand up to his lips and kisses the warmth back into her palm. "That's another one. You are magic, my love."

My love. Jesper Idyll just called her his love.

The cold, the wet, the terror—it melts away like cotton candy in the rain. She is warm now, glowing with happiness and a shy sort of triumph. What she feels, what he makes her feel—he really does feel it, too.

Jesper stands and reaches down, pulling her to her feet. Holding both her hands, he walks backward toward the cross, pulling her along. "It's honestly so easy. Have you done any acting?"

"In high school..."

"I told you that," Solomon reminds him.

"So, yeah. We'll drag you in through the door. Fight us. Not violently—like, don't hit or kick anyone—but lots of pulling. You don't want to go. You can make any sounds you like, because the music will be the only thing you hear, once we've done all the mixing. We'll force your wrists into the manacles—they're lined, so it shouldn't hurt, and you thrash for a minute. I'll put my hand to your forehead, and you go stock still, and when I pull my hand away, you kind of collapse. Like Maria was, when you showed up."

It seems easy enough. But...

"What comes after that?"

"That's as far as we want to get tonight. We're still working on the rest of it, but this will let us get started."

Nico appears wearing his Buddha smile. "I told her we were done filming for the night and sent her back home. Are we a go?"

They all look to her.

Black Idyll.

The band.

The greatest band in the world.

They look to her.

Hope, eagerness, friendliness.

They want this.

They want *her*.

They want her to be a part of the magic they create.

She looks down, stunned and humbled.

"OK, but can you see through my gown? Because I'm not down for that part."

They all laugh, and Nico goes to fetch some pasties from—somewhere—and then Angelina is poised outside the door. The boys—she will always think of them as boys, rather than men, because she began loving them when they were boys—they tie on their cloaks and put on their masks. Now that she knows who they are, she can see how each mask suits its wearer, how these, too, are works of art, the lost boys playing dress up. She's always loved this about Black Idyll, how everything has always meant something, layers and layers of metaphor and callbacks and throughlines. She wrote a ten-page paper on imagery and symbolism comparing their song "Daggersmile" to *Macbeth* back in high school and got a 105.

"We're ready," Manny says, his voice muffled by the rabbit mask as he moves from camera to camera like a humming-bird. "Recording is on."

Nico starts the song on his phone, the same song Angelina followed to this room.

Jesper looks to her—or, more accurately, the unicorn head cocks to face her. Up close, this one is quite different from the one at the rave and outside her house tonight. The shape, the colors, the details—it was made to match the other three masks as a series, stylized and elegant, while there is something rough and grotesque about the other—

Well, she's not going to think about that right now.

She must've dreamed it.

Everything about tonight's balcony encounter was

impossible, but it brought her here, and this is a dream come true. If she goes back home tomorrow morning by the light of day and sees massive, gray wet spots on her ceiling and wet footprints across her room, then she'll know for certain that it was real. And if not, she'll know something else.

"Ready in three, two, one," Manny says quietly.

Jesper clutches one wrist while Solomon takes the other. Their fingers are firm but not cruel, and as they pull her from the hall and through the door, she fights like a rebellious pony. Not kicking and screaming, but rearing and pulling, plunging and twisting, teeth gritted. Her wet hair flies in her face, slaps across the masks. Nico is behind her, pushing, while Manny waits at the door.

"Perfect," Jesper whispers. "You're doing great."

The door shuts softly, and then Manny stands beside the big X, rabbit ears regally high as the others pull her toward it. She gasps as if seeing it for the first time and rears back, doing her best to pantomime the fear she felt earlier as her friends drag her inexorably across the room, past the candelabras, across the rich rugs.

But—

Something—

They want—

Fear falls over her like a shadow, and her muscles tense.

They are leading her to a cage, a prison, a torture instrument, a slaughter.

It's not real, she knows that, but it *is* real, those manacles are real, and once her wrists are in them, anything could happen.

Anything.

When she tries to pull away this time, it is with such sudden intensity that her arm snaps out of Solomon's fingers. Emboldened, she spins to run, but Jesper pulls her back violently, jerking across the room. Solomon's hands clamp down around her forearm as Nico sinks his nails into her shoulders, forcing her forward. She bucks and rears, muttering, "No, no, please no," but they don't stop, they keep pulling, they keep pushing, they only hold her all the harder.

And then she's at the big X, and she can smell fresh-cut wood, oil, leather. It feels like dozens of fingers wrap around her left arm as they force it upward, and she fights it with everything in her, teeth gritted, but then the cuff is around her flesh and Manny is buckling it so tightly that her fingers are already going cold. Her right hand follows while her brain is still catching up to the reality of being captured. Another buckle, and her arms are spread and shackled overhead, her fingers numb, and the men step back in their terrifying masks to silently survey their grim work. She thrashes and tugs, pulls and screams, and the unicorn mask cocks to the side like an alien trying to understand an animal. A hand reaches out, the cold palm flat against her forehead.

"You are mine," someone says.

Her fingers curl into fists and her head hangs. Behind the ragged wall of her hair, she is crying.

She let them do this.

She trusted them.

What has she done?

Maybe a ghost is what we need.
The living aren't giving, they're
    full of greed.
When you've already lost, when
    you're already gone.
A queen can never be a pawn.
Fall in love, fall to your knees
Her hive is filled with adoring
    bees
Each sting kills not one but two
Each sting kills both me and you

"THE STING THAT KILLS," UNRELEASED,
FROM THE PERSONAL COLLECTION OF JESPER IDYLL.

19

"And... cut!" Manny says.

Laughter and high fives occur somewhere far away, and then big, warm hands unbuckle the manacles and massage feeling back into Angelina's numb fingers.

"That was perfect!" Jesper says. "Flawless! Baby, that was so damn good!"

The masks are off again, the cloaks shed in a shadowy pile of satin. Manny and Nico are watching footage on a video camera with wild grins as Solomon puts out candles one by one with an old-fashioned brass candle snuffer shaped like a golden leopard. When each flame dies, there's a tiny hiss and the stink of smoke. Angelina slowly returns to her body. She is shaking again as she brushes tangled hair out of her face.

Jesper doesn't seem to notice that she's one step away from dissociating. He gathers her into a hug and twirls her around, planting a tender kiss on her temple.

"Incredible," he says wonderingly. "You were the missing

piece." He looks up. "Guys, we're going to bed. Good work. See you in the morning."

The others mutter their compliments and goodbyes and continue their work cleaning up from playing at ritual sacrifice. Jesper puts his arm around Angelina's waist and guides her to his room. This is the first time she's seen it less than spotlessly clean; a large suitcase is open on the floor, spilling far more clothes, skinny scarves, and boots than anyone in the world could possibly use in four days. With heartbreaking normalcy, Jesper Idyll strips out of his white velvet tuxedo jacket and hangs it up on a wooden hanger. He steps out of his crisp white trousers and shakes out the wrinkles before slipping them onto another hanger. Standing there in a white Goblin King blouse and black boxer briefs, he runs fingers through his hair and rubs the black charcoal around his eyes, looking like nothing so much as a tired little boy up way past his bedtime on Halloween. He is staggeringly beautiful, perfect, an angel made flesh, and Angelina sits on his bed and tucks her knees up to her chin. The storm outside has ended, but the storm in her heart rages on.

"There was a man on my balcony," she says in a tiny voice. "A naked man in a unicorn mask. But it wasn't you."

His head jerks to look at her, his eyes alert now. "Definitely not me. On your balcony? How could someone get on your balcony?"

"I... I don't know. I woke up when the storm got bad and there he was. That's why I ran here. That's why I had Nico's knife. I was scared."

Jesper is immediately on the bed by her side, taking her hand. "I'm so sorry. That must've been terrifying."

"It was."

"Why didn't you say anything? When you got here? We should go look for him. If we have a trespasser, that's a serious problem."

She wraps her fingers around his, making a ball of their hands, her knees turned to touch his. "Because maybe... I dreamed it? The ceiling was leaking. But not just rain—it was gray, almost black. Like ink. And the balcony door was locked—I locked it—but he opened it. Once I got here and saw you, it just felt too ridiculous to be real."

Because so many things feel unreal at the House of Idyll, don't they? She lives here for free, she is fed gourmet meals, she is given everything she needs, she does yoga with rock stars. Hell, she was just in a music video harkening back to Black Idyll's very first number one hit, "Un1c0rn," which she's seen at least a million times.

And now she is in bed with Jesper Idyll.

Not the slick, polished rock star, but the guy who gets his head caught and breaks out laughing when he tries to pull off his frilly blouse. Not the runway model who won't walk without sunglasses but the shy boy who still chews his painted fingernails down to the quick when he's nervous.

She gets to see the side of Jesper that he protects from the world. Secret, tender, childlike. Everyone else can watch him on *The View*, but Angelina gets to make a pillow fort and drink cocoa with the real Jesper while they watch horror movies from the eighties and scream warnings at the screen.

"Fear isn't ridiculous." He looks down at their hands and kisses her fingers one by one. "Dreams are the mind's playground, and even nightmares have stories to tell. Storms have their own magic. Stay here with me tonight, and in the morning, we'll go make sure your place is safe. If not, we'll move you in here, if you like. There are plenty of rooms." He nuzzles their hands, then gets up to make sure that his door is locked. He checks the sliding glass door to the balcony and the windows, looks in the massive bathroom and the massive closet and under the massive bed.

"No monsters," he says with an understanding smile. "Promise."

From that moment on, everything is sweet. Jesper offers her boxers and a T-shirt, since she's still damp. He turns on the bed heater and tucks her in and pulls her against his body. He's so lithe that she sometimes forgets how muscular he is, how much time he spends in the gym at the Well. The cage of his arms will keep her safe; the bastion of his body will stand like a seawall between Angelina and the monsters that howl for her in the midst of the storm.

"You were magnificent tonight," he murmurs into her hair. And sometime later, when she's about to fall off the cliff into sleep, "I think I might love you."

She carries his words with her, carries them like armor into the darkness, and when she wakes, sun streams in through the window and Jesper Idyll is gazing at her with fondness and wonder. He offers her a fluffy white robe, and they stumble downstairs to find Nico making waffles in the kitchen. Manny returns from the Well with a mountain of fresh fruit while Solomon uses a complicated machine to make velvety black coffee. Angelina is an only child, but this feels like a family breakfast, the boys all familiar and fond and her comfortable among them, easy as pie. They've all done a poor job removing the thick black eyeshadow from around their eyes; they look less like rock stars and more like they've been playing at ghosts or zombies. She eats and chats and laughs, and then Jesper offers to escort her home and make sure she'll be safe there.

This is not the walk of shame—it's more like a walk of pride. She is wearing Jesper Idyll's white clothes and someone's oversized white Crocs as they stroll hand in hand through a beautiful morning of sunshine and sparkling dewdrops. Her tiny house looks perfectly normal from the outside. She walks to the edge of the forest to look for hoofprints, but the ground is soup and cluttered with fallen leaves and branches.

"You said he was on the balcony?" Jesper asks. He stands at her porch, looking up, trying to puzzle out how a naked man might parkour his way up to the second story. It seems impossible, but then again, lots of things do.

"Yes. He was outside in the storm, and then he came inside, and I ran."

Her front door is unlocked, as she left it, and within, she is startled to find not a single item out of place. She is quite certain she flung open drawers and cabinets, hunting for a weapon, but everything is neatly closed. There are no muddy footprints, not a single drop of water. Upstairs, the ceiling is unblemished, her bed unmade but clean and dry. Even the sliding glass door is locked from the inside and doesn't have a handprint. She breathes hot air onto the glass, expecting to see the greasy kiss of an unnaturally long hand, but there is nothing.

"I guess it was a dream," she says, half relieved and half embarrassed.

Jesper draws her against his chest. "Good," he says. "Good."

He heads back up to the big house to work on the video with the guys, and Angelina locks her door and takes a shower and puts on her own clothes and sits down at her little kitchen table with her laptop. Before she can write, she always goes through a loop of tabs, checking her email addresses and doing word games and seeing if BuzzFeed has any good articles about the stupid shit guys say on Bumble. But today, a news headline catches her eyes.

MARIA PEREZ, PRINCIPAL DANCER OF THE CUBAN BALLET AND EX-GIRLFRIEND OF BLACK IDYLL'S JESPER IDYLL FOUND DEAD.

The nights are long,
    but life is short
This death is not a petite mort
Live big, live fast, die young,
    it's past
Your days are numbered, time is vast
To brightly shine take my advice
Crave the glory, pay the price

"LOVE SONG OF THE MOTH," TRACK #3 ON
BLACK IDYLL, THE SUCCULENT REAPING.
KAKOPHONY RECORDS, 2024.

20

Angelina has never clicked on anything so quickly in her life. There is a photo of the interior of a hotel room at Chateau Marmont with the middle pixelated, but there is obviously a lot of blood in that bed.

A *lot* of blood.

Maria Perez was found by hotel staff at 11:43 a.m. this morning in her room at Chateau Marmont. After attending the Grammys last night and making an appearance at a few after-parties, Ms. Perez returned to the hotel at 4:12 a.m. An anonymous source says, "She'd been crying. Her mascara was crazy, and her hair was messed up. She was carrying her Louboutins." According to staff, Ms. Perez waved away an offer of help and went directly to her room. There were no noise reports or calls to the front desk, nor did anyone else enter her room, according to security footage. When Ms. Perez did not check out this morning as expected, staff entered her room and, sadly, discovered her body. Authorities are requesting any information that might help in better understanding what happened to Ms. Perez, as the circumstances of her cause of death are highly unusual.

The article is accompanied by a picture of Maria laughing on the red carpet in a gorgeous, fire-engine-red dress, sleeveless with a huge skirt. Angelina realizes she has never seen Maria in anything but white, and red suits her so much better. She wishes she could see what the pixelation hides in the image. Did Maria... slit her wrists, like Megan did? Nico made it sound like she didn't even know she'd been fired, but obviously she was distraught. She must've gone directly from House of Idyll to her hotel, and then...

Well, did something to herself.

Something with a lot of blood.

This does not seem like the sort of thing Maria would do, but then again, Angelina has only known her for a few weeks, and even then only peripherally. The main thing she knows about Maria, actually, is that the woman absolutely craves attention. Her wardrobe, her makeup, her big laugh, her habit of doing ballet in non-ballet settings. Angelina could see her having a very public, melodramatic breakdown, the sort of thing that would send Jesper scurrying back to her, that would get her in the news, but she can't see Maria marring herself. She's too proud. Too vain.

Or was.

At least, that's how Angelina sees it.

There's no way Maria would destroy the temple of her

body in private with no audience and no chance of survival, and especially with no chance of a contrite Jesper Idyll knocking on her door with white roses.

Then again...

After a little more internet sleuthing, Angelina finds it. The photo of Maria, but without the pixelation. The gossip rag must've paid an enormous amount for it, and it's highly likely that it will be removed shortly because it's so goddamn graphic and grim. Angelina takes a screen shot, then blows the image up to try and understand what's happening.

Maria did not slit her wrists.

Maria sliced off her face.

Her body is nude, splayed out awkwardly on the king-sized bed.

But her face, her beautiful face—

It's gone.

The skin is gone. Her dark eyes stare unblinking like fat grapes nestled into shiny pink meat. Her ears are still there, her hairline is still there, but from her forehead to her chin, the skin has been ripped away to expose the viscera underneath.

That's when Angelina understands that there's literally no way Maria could've done this. She would never harm her face, even if a human being had the capability to— to—

Skin themselves alive.

Someone else did this.

There is no weapon visible, just what's left of Maria and the blood that's seeped out—

Oh.

And a stab wound.

Right in the middle of her belly.

Her face is so, so... compelling that Angelina didn't even notice.

She looks to her door, checks that it is locked.

Whoever did this to Maria is still out there.

They are not on the cameras at the most exclusive hotel in the world.

They are out there, and they are dangerous.

Angelina can't help wondering if... maybe... the man in the unicorn mask followed Maria home? Maybe he hid in the trunk of her car? Maybe he drove her? Angelina wants to know if Maria took an Uber, if she had a limo. How did she get from here, where she was supposedly happy and laughing, to there, where she was murdered in the most horrible, violent way possible?

At least it wasn't the band, Angelina thinks. She was with them the whole time. All four of them.

Of course, there are still forty other people at the compound, plus the staff, who are mostly invisible but apparently treated well and paid generously. Cleaners and cooks and a weathered old handyman who lives twenty minutes away and drives over whenever anything needs fixing.

Oh no.

Does Jesper know?

She throws on a sweater and hurries back to the big house. In the kitchen, she finds a woman in a white uniform cleaning up Nico's breakfast mess.

"Do you know where they are?" Angelina asks her.

The woman's look is blank. "They don't tell me anything. Sorry."

For the second time today, Angelina explores the house, looking for signs of life. She can't find anyone, only evidence of their passing. Then she remembers: they were going to work on the video. They're probably in the studio. It's in an old barn off to the side, and she's never had reason to go there before. The band maintains a level of separation from House of Idyll; they participate when they wish but they refuse to be inconvenienced or bothered when they are doing the work that sustains them all. Maybe she should just text Jesper — or the Inner Circle?

Which would be easier if she'd brought her phone. It used to make her feel connected, but now that she has actual, daily connections with everyone at House of Idyll, she doesn't crave the constant hum of doomscrolling. The outside world is almost distasteful, the thought of a horrible boss dressing her down or her mom randomly calling to make suggestions about her life feels as foreign as something that happens on Mars. She has everything she needs here. Friends, art, health, activity, maybe love. Still, it would be nice if she could check the group chat right now and see if the others know about Maria.

Angelina stands at the door to the white barn. The Black Idyll unicorn crest has been stenciled onto the old wood, and when she places her hand over it, she can feel the thump of music inside. It's a new song but somewhat familiar; they must've played it at the rave, or maybe while filming the video.

Hating the way they looked at her when she interrupted the shoot, she waits until the song is over and quiet reigns before opening the door.

She's in a sort of lounge done up in shades of white and cream with tons of shag carpet and sheepskin, and through a shaded glass she sees the band circled around a bunch of machinery she doesn't understand, talking to a sound guy who's grinning like he just won the lottery.

"Who's that?" he says when he notices her staring.

The band glares at her and Manny mutters something with a sneer before Jesper hurries through several doors to where Angelina stands in the softest room in the world feeling horribly small and exposed and stupid, like she doesn't belong here at all.

"What?" he asks sharply.

He has never spoken to her like this, never shown her anything but kindness, tenderness, passion, and joy. She's uncertain but quickly regains her confidence. "Did you hear about Maria?" she asks.

That only makes him more annoyed. He stamps a foot. "No. Is she throwing another tantrum? Did she do a podcast?"

"She's dead."

He blinks at her, annoyance bleeding into shock. "What?"

"They found her in her hotel room this morning."

"Prove it."

Angelina holds out her empty hands. "I didn't bring my phone. But it's everywhere, if you have yours."

Jesper pulls his phone out of his pocket and after a few

taps, all the color drains from his face. His jaw is working, his breathing fast.

"This isn't possible," he murmurs.

"Jesper, I looked it up. I saw the— the whole photo. Someone did this to her. They ripped her face off. The skin. Gone. They stabbed her."

His eyes close, and a single tear falls down his sharp cheekbone. "Why are you telling me this?"

She aches to touch him, but he is holding himself away, barely holding himself together. "Because I didn't want you to find out—"

"No! Why are you telling me— the details? Why did you even look?"

She swallows. "Because I'm scared. What if the guy in the unicorn mask—"

His finger is in her face, cutting her off. "No. No. Your stupid nightmare did not kill Maria. That's insane. You imagined something, and... They're not connected. Just go away. Let me deal with this."

Angelina can't stop the shuddering sob that claws its way out of her throat. She swallows it down and turns. She does not look in his eyes again, doesn't attempt to touch him or change his mind. This version of Jesper—hard, cold, cruel. She wants nothing to do with it. She glances briefly at the other guys in the sound booth, and they might as well be wearing their masks again. Their faces are guarded, closed. These are not the people who giggled as they threw raspberries at each other at breakfast. These are strangers.

Outside, the bright day feels dull, the colors muted. Angelina walks back to her little house with her head held high, using every muscle in her body to will herself not to cry.

"Hey, Angelina! Do you know—"

She walks right past Thierry, just shakes her head the smallest bit.

She doesn't know anything anymore.

She knows that she saw what she saw last night, and she knows it wasn't real. She knows that Maria Perez is dead. She knows that Jesper is childishly channeling his grief about that death onto her, immaturely punishing her with his pain. She can't change any of these things. All she can do is feel like an open wound.

Her phone has dozens of messages in the regular House of Idyll group chat and the Inner Circle group chat. She ignores them. There's no way anything could make her feel better right now, and plenty of things could make her feel worse. She sits at her laptop, but the music won't come. She tries napping, reading, even picks up on her failed crochet attempt from Craft Night, but nothing can distract her. Instead, she decides to go for a walk. She puts on her sturdiest shoes and heads out to the lake. The path meanders, the sculptures unmoving in the still air. The magic, for now, lies dead.

When the forest opens up to reveal the beach, a dark lump mars the sweeping vista. Something brown, covered in shifting black.

A horse.

A palomino.

Maybe one of the ones she thought she saw in the storm.

It's crawling with vultures.

She edges closer out of grim curiosity, and the vultures spread their dark wings and croak and caw, protecting their treasure. The horse's belly is open to the sky, its viscera glistening and pink and speckled with sand. It's so recent it doesn't smell yet. Even the flies have not arrived.

"So much death," Angelina mutters to herself.

She turns around, leaving the vultures to their feast. Normally, she would alert someone to this public health hazard, but Angelina is done being the bearer of bad news. Punish the messenger and they stop carrying the messages. Let Nico drag everyone out here for a drum circle of grief and smell it himself.

Angelina stops by the Well and indiscriminately throws food into a net bag. People call her name, ask her questions, invite her to sit, but she can only shake her head and mumble apologies. She has lots of acquaintances but no genuine friends. It's a startling realization about life at House of Idyll. When you give someone everything they need to survive, they have no reason to form strong bonds. This is a community without a community. There is no horrible boss whose cruelty brings employees together in unified hatred. There is no need to borrow a cup of sugar, no reason to return an emptied Tupperware that once held chicken soup. When people don't need each other, they don't need each other, but that only makes them need each other more.

At the door, Angelina turns and looks back at all the artists and models and musicians and podcasters and writers grouped together as they eat pasture-raised organic chicken over quinoa hash. She only knows half their names. She doesn't know anyone's favorite color or if they have kids or where their pets are while they're living life in this luxury compound. And they don't know anything real about her, either.

She's outside now, but she turns back around to peek in the window. Could one of these men be the guy in the unicorn mask? He was white and thin and tall, very pale with no tattoos and no body hair, which significantly cuts down the possible subjects. That leaves maybe three guys. Thierry, Chris, and Marcus. She can't imagine any of them donning a unicorn mask and standing around naked in the rain.

But maybe—

Maybe the mask is in someone's studio or house. It has to be somewhere. Of course, if the guy in the unicorn mask is the one who hurt Maria, he would go to pains to hide it. Or maybe—

No. There's no way.

Naked guys in big horse masks can't just walk into Chateau Marmont and then waltz out covered in blood and holding flaps of human face.

The guy in the mask at the rave was Jesper. The guy in the mask on her balcony in the rain was a nightmare. And whatever happened to Maria happened an hour away, long after she'd left this place. It was strange and tragic, but strange and tragic shit happens all the time. Being beautiful and talented and famous doesn't inoculate anyone from suffering. There's no point in trying to connect the dots.

Back in her house, Angelina builds a nest in her bed and watches baking shows on her laptop while she eats cheese and crackers and organic fruit and single-origin dark chocolate truffles, the closest thing to junk food offered by House of Idyll. She hasn't seen a single packaged product here that wasn't Idyllic brand, no corn syrup or artificial colors. She would kill for a bag of Cheetos, for fingers roughly coated in orange powder.

As she watches an old Englishman attempt a rough puff pastry, she hears something outside. Not a storm, not rogue horses, not a creepy freak spreading sticky frog fingers against her window.

It's music.

It's Jesper Idyll, singing.

You are magic, tragic, the one I need
You are my blood, the air I breathe
You see the truth amidst the lies
A glittering moth among butterflies
Every artist needs a seed
You're in my lungs, the air I breathe
Angeline, Angeline,
Prettiest angel I've ever seen

"DARK ANGEL," UNRELEASED, FROM THE
PERSONAL COLLECTION OF JESPER IDYLL.

21

Angelina stands on her porch, tearstained, staring at a beautiful boy with a guitar. Jesper looks up at her, barefoot in the grass, wearing his white tux from the Grammys, playing an old, cheap, beat-to-hell acoustic guitar as he sings.

To her.

A new song, one she's never heard before.

A song *about* her.

She could convince herself otherwise except he used her name.

Well, he actually changed it a little.

Now it fits the fucking rhyme scheme.

His voice is so pure, so gentle, so soft. Most of his songs are bellowed or screamed, shivering with rage. A few ballads are sad and plaintive. But this is almost shy, heartbreakingly sweet. His eyes meet hers, and even from ten feet away she could dive into those blue pools, crisp and clear as a cenote. He looks tired, she thinks, purple smudges under his long lashes and his hair more mussed than usual. The song ends with a final chorus, and he flips the guitar onto his back, the ratty black velvet strap bisecting his tux jacket. He ducks his head, hands in his pockets.

"That's my first playthrough," he says. "But I know all the lines by heart."

It dawns on her that this is his version of an apology.

For what happened in the barn.

He was angry and hurt, and she could see at the time that he was projecting, but now she wonders if this poor, broken boy even knows how real people make amends. He couldn't find the right words, so instead he wrote an entire goddamn song, words and notes and a fucking bridge. If it were anyone else in the world, it would be time to sit down and discuss open lines of communication, but Jesper Idyll has just written a song for her and played it on his first guitar from way back when, from when he was nothing, and she is so touched, so over-whelmed, that all she can do is throw herself into his arms. His wiry strength, as always, surprises her. The spare hardness of his chest against her cheek, the solid scaffold of his arms, the point of his chin tucked over her forehead.

"I'm sorry," he whispers. "I was cruel. You didn't deserve that."

"You were scared and hurt," she whispers back. "And it sucked. But I get it."

He pulls away, tips her head back. Their eyes meet, and her body comes alive with the thrill of diving into a cold pool on a hot summer day, a delicious but welcome and familiar shock.

"Do you forgive me?" he asks.

He... really does need to know. She can see the worry between his brows, the clenching in his jaw.

"Of course. Do you know more? Do they know who—"

He shakes his head. "I know what you know, and I don't want to talk about it. Dwelling too deeply on tragedy only causes more tragedy. What is done can't be undone. All we can do is move on. Maria... she had a rough past. She was in a lot of pain, but now her soul is free."

"Does everyone here have a rough past?"

His look is fond as he smooths back her hair, running his fingers through it and filling her with shivers. "Of course. That's what makes us artists. The greater your pain, the greater your capacity for passion and joy. Speaking of which..." His fingers gently tug the ends of her long hair. "Would you consider singing with us in the studio? We have a song on the new album and... I want you. *We* want you. Your voice. It's perfect."

Angelina trembles like she might crawl out of her own skin. This is the happiest moment of her life. The thing she's always wanted. The thing she's been waiting for, hoping for, but too scared to ask for. Not only because it will give her a credit that will help her build a real career on her own, not only because it will give her access to people in the business, but mainly because she wants to feel her voice meld with Jesper's, with the powerhouse of sound that is Black Idyll, her favorite band from the moment she heard "Un1c0rn" when she was fourteen.

"Of course." She is struggling so hard to remain cool that she deserves an award. "That sounds great."

Jesper's face lights up, and he leans in to kiss her gently on the lips. "Great. Perfect. Are you open today? We're on a short timeline."

It is laughable that he thinks there is literally anything in the world she would rather do.

"I'm open."

His thumb presses at the corner of her lips as he kisses her again. "I'll give you some time to get ready. Meet me at the studio in an hour? I, uh, I promise I'll be much nicer this time."

She nods, smiling into his eyes, and he traces his fingers down the chain of her necklace and rubs his finger over the unicorn pendant at her throat before casually strolling away barefoot in a couture white tux with the guitar slung on his back like the bard from some ancient tale of heroes.

Angelina wants to whoop and scream, but tiny houses have thin walls. She hurries inside to shower, dry her hair straight, do her brows—God, she is so giddy it's insane. She heads to the Well to pick out a fresh new dress and a white ribbon for her hair; she sings better with it pulled out of her face. On the way back to her house, she stops in the garden to pluck mint and sage and licorice to mix with the organic honey she's already drizzled heavily into her mug. She remembers how she used to feel excluded from the garden, but now Marnie and Lisbon are deferential, sweet. Angelina is in the Inner Circle, chosen by Jesper Idyll himself, and that carries power here. As she walks back out of the labyrinth of greenery, she passes a freshly dug bed, the dark earth overturned in three long rows, ready for seeds or seedlings. She'd hoped to work out here once, to learn about growing things and keeping them alive, but she has other, more lofty concerns.

Back home, she sips her tea and sings scales as she waits for an email or a text, some glimpse of the song she's to sing. Nothing arrives. Don't they want her to practice, or at least have some familiarity with the notes?

Ah, well. They have been a world-renowned professional band for ten years. They know what they're doing better than she does.

Exactly one hour later, Angelina stands before the barn. The door is open this time, and when she enters the plush white room, everyone is glad to see her. Well, maybe not Manny. He's the one she knows the least, the one who seems to hold himself apart from the community here; they've never even had a conversation. Manny smiles at her, but his eyes are troubled.

Solomon pulls her into a hug, laughing and muttering, "I told you so, love," in that delectable voice of his. Nico beams and pats her on the back. And Jesper holds out a pair of headphones and beckons her to a microphone.

"Sorry I couldn't send it. We have to keep things extremely secret. Very analog. Look this over and see if it makes sense. Or if it needs changes."

It's laughable, that she might have notes for Jesper Idyll, but she appreciates his attempt at humility.

He hands her a piece of staff paper with notes carefully inked in black, the words underneath them in Jesper's block lettering. It's a back-and-forth, two beasts calling across a starlit valley, and she immediately understands that this is the song that will go with the video she helped them film.

"It's perfect," she says, because it is. Jesper's songs are brilliant, and this one is no different. It fits with the band's dark aesthetic, the poetic themes of sacrifice and transformation. She doesn't have many lines, but she is not the star here, and she knows it.

Angelina is about to find out if their voices merge as beautifully as their bodies and minds, and she has never been so ready for anything in all her life.

Jesper puts on his headphones and nods at her to do the same. Nico sits at the drums, kicks and swats and tests, spins a drumstick around one finger. Solomon holds his bass like a lover, checking its tune with his eyes closed and his hips pressed forward. Manny barks orders at the sound guys sitting at a bank of controls and scowls as he adjusts a tuning peg.

The studio goes silent, oppressively so. Jesper nods at Nico, who stands, hits his drumsticks three times over his head, and shouts, "One, two, one two three four!"

And then the music is happening. She was expecting it to be rough, but it is flawless. They have practiced it before, many times — or maybe they're just that good, a well-oiled machine of professionals after all these years. The sound fills her head, pouring in from the headphones, pure and true and loud. She watches the sheet Jesper holds between them, and then his voice purrs into her ears and she answers like she's been silent all her life until this very moment, her heart gone staccato and her eyes tearing up with the pure joy of it all as she harmonizes and responds.

This is the song that binds with blood
The flower burst from swollen bud
Old bones arisen, flecked with dew
Do you give yourself to me?
I do.

The time has come, the time has gone
The stag who waits was once a fawn
Everything I say is true
Do you give yourself to me?
I do.

The beast within me hungers, cries
To swallow tongue and heart and eyes
The sky is dark, the moon is new
Do you give yourself to me?
I do.

The thunderous one who bends the trees
Will make a blushing bride of thee
Thrice has he claimed his crimson due
Do you give yourself to me?
I do.

He's at the door, impatient, hard
The abattoir his calling card

The pact between us will renew
Do you give yourself to me?
I do.

No creature him of woman born
Great King with claws and rampant horn
Here he comes, he's stepping through
Do you give yourself to him?
I do.

The last word draws out, and she wonders if they will have violinists layered in for the final cut. When the sound guy gives them the okay, she turns to Jesper.

"So how was that?" she asks, absolutely fishing for a compliment because she is singing with the most talented musician in the world.

His eyes glow, his smile wide. "It was perfect. You were perfect."

"So are we going again?"

He chuckles. "Why? We nailed it in one."

That... does not seem right. She's read that most recording sessions involve at least three takes, if not more, plus breaking down some sections. Then again, maybe they use auto-tune and other tools to nudge everything into the right direction.

And yet...

"Seriously? Because I know I was flat at least twice. And I know you heard it."

Jesper waves that way. "They'll fix it in post."

"Let's get one more," Solomon says, velvety and easygoing. "Just to make sure."

He gives Jesper a look she can't read, and Jesper shrugs, and Nico counts them in again. She's so much better this time; she knows the song, is familiar with the timing and the words. She'd love a third try, but everyone agrees two is fine for now. They might call her back in later, but for today, this is a triumph.

"And we have something special planned," Jesper says, once he's removed her headphones. "We'd like to take you out to dinner. To thank you. If this song does what we think it will do, it's all due to you. And I've booked you some time here next week, if you'd like to record some of your work for a demo. If you're ready."

Angelina feels her cheeks go red. This is all so much. Is it legal for one person to get everything they've ever wanted, to be this happy in one short day? She briefly remembers how the morning began and feels a wash of guilt, but...

Maybe Jesper is right. Hasn't she known enough hardship? Why dwell on something she can't change? She barely knew Maria. What's done is done.

They step outside to find Mr. B waiting in a white stretch limo, the kind Angelina is quite certain no one uses these days outside of proms and weddings. They pile in, and Solomon pops a bottle of Dom and passes her a glass coupe filled with bubbles.

"To Angelina!" Jesper says, holding his glass aloft.

"To Angelina!" the band repeats, and they drink, and Angelina's head goes swimmy.

It's an hour's ride into LA, where she hasn't been in, what? Months? Ever since Solomon whisked her away from a daily grind that was mostly worry and work with very little breathing room for happiness or art. She has been living the life of her dreams, and this opportunity—singing with Black Idyll—will launch her directly into her future.

They pull up to Nobu in Malibu and are escorted to a patio table overlooking the ocean. As the sun sets, they drink more champagne and begin an eight-course omakase adventure. Angelina has grown accustomed to high quality sushi and sashimi in her time at House of Idyll, but she has never experienced food this incredible. Her taste buds are alight, her head spinning. She is food drunk, life drunk, champagne drunk. She is laughing with Black Idyll, she is kissing Jesper with salt-crusted lips, she is high on life and wonders if things could possibly ever be better than this.

"They can," Jesper whispers in her ear. "There is no limit to joy."

She— did she say that out loud?

God, she needs to slow down on the champagne.

It's kind of difficult when her glass is always magically refilled.

She's so full now that she can barely breathe, so happy all she can do is laugh. They leave in a rowdy pack, Jesper's arm around her. Flashbulbs go off outside, and—

Of course.

Paparazzi.

She's never had to deal with them before because she's

never left House of Idyll with the band. If things continue in this fashion, she'll have to get used to this kind of treatment, loud men squatting behind bushes and shouting at her, shoving cameras into her face.

"Jesper, who's the girl?"

"Jesper, is the band doing a ten-year anniversary tour next year?"

"Jesper, it's been a decade since Vivian died. Will there be a tribute?"

"Jesper, how can you celebrate on the day your ex-girlfriend was found murdered?"

Jesper nods at Nico, and Nico punches that guy's camera, knocking it directly into his eye and landing him on the concrete on his back.

They dive in the limo, and Mr. B peels out to a blinding chorus of flashbulbs.

"We're going to pay for that," Manny mutters.

"It won't matter," Solomon reminds him. "It never does."

For a few minutes, they are silent and somber, and then Solomon pops open another bottle of champagne. "Fuck it. We celebrate life!" he shouts. "We celebrate passion and art and all that is idyllic!"

They toast and drink and Jesper pulls Angelina into his lap and kisses her until the world dissolves.

"This is the best night of my life," she murmurs.

His grin is a deliciously salacious thing. "And it's not over yet," he promises.

All my life I've wanted something more
More than just ceilings, walls, and a floor
Day and night are a fight, sick of being poor
Ugly crying, sobbing, sighing, what's it all for?
So when the time comes, when it's all on the line
I will pull up my chair, take up my knife and dine
All the world will watch me sip the finest wine
Swear to give it my all, so all will be mine
Can anyone be ready when the time is right?
On your mark, get set, it's time to fight
My blood pumps red, my soul is white
Everything begins when it starts tonight

"SONG OF BECOMING," TRACK #10 ON BLACK IDYLL,
THE SUCCULENT REAPING, KAKOPHONY RECORDS, 2024.

22

Back at the villa, Jesper swings a stumbling Angelina into his arms and carries her over the threshold like a gallant groom with his blushing bride. The rest of the band disappears as they pass by the unicorn statue and head up the stairs. Jesper's breath is hot in her ear as he breathes, "God, how I crave you. I have never wanted anything so badly in my life. You were perfect. You've been perfect."

How is he even upright, she wonders? They have been drinking steadily for hours. She can barely stand, and yet he can carry her upstairs. Rock-star tolerance, must be. He pauses at a closed door, kissing along her ear and down her neck, sending rivulets of pleasure radiating through her entire body.

"Can we try something different?" he asks, dark and seductive. "Something I've been fantasizing about?"

Jesper Idyll... has been fantasizing about her.

This should be no surprise. They've slept together multiple times, seen each other naked, seen every inch of each other, and yet she doubts this will ever get old.

"What'd you have in mind?"

It comes out a little slurred, and she feels the smallest pinch of shame, but, well, who gives a fuck? She sang on an album today. She partied with musical gods who fed her the best champagne money can buy. Her job, basically, was to get smashed.

Jesper sets her lightly on her feet, walking her backward until she's against the wall. He leans close, tracing gentle fingertips down her bare arms until they reach her wrists. Lifting them over her head and gathering them both into one hand, he grinds his hips against hers and whispers hot breath into her ear.

"I want to tie you up and make you come until you scream my name."

Angelina sucks in a breath, her insides molten and aching.

"How can I say no to that?"

His smile is carnal, hungry, confident, and she would do anything he asked right now. "Wait here," he whispers.

She leans against the wall as the hallway spins around her, and then Jesper is back and sliding a silky mask down over her eyes. He takes her hands and leads her forward, helping her sit on something unfamiliar and soft. She has been in this house dozens of times but can't remember where she is, where anything is. With gentle care, Jesper removes her sandals, kissing her toes and massaging her arches. He helps her stand and steadies her shoulders before lifting the long white dress off over her head. The room is warm, the air still, almost cocoon-like. She'd like to make a joke about being glad she shaved, but there is something reverential in Jesper's treatment tonight that holds her tongue. This is special, she thinks, more so than usual.

She means something to him, and he's showing her that.

He brought her into the recording studio, he sang with her, he took her to dinner with the band, he was photographed with her. She thought the Inner Circle was the best she could ever hope for, but now, at least for tonight, she is one of them. She is part of Black Idyll, part of the thing that saved her when she was a lost and broken teenager, the words that built the scaffold around which she constructed her adult self from the wrecked ruins of a neglected and misunderstood childhood.

She is standing in nothing but white panties and a silver unicorn pendant as the world dizzily whirls around her, struggling to keep her balance as everything in existence conspires to muddle her senses. She is a creature of pure sensation, lost in utter darkness.

If only she were more sober.

She wants so badly to please him.

Somewhere, fabric falls to the floor. Jesper is undressing. She wishes she could see the fine, beautiful bones of him, the ropey muscle, the fluttering lines along his ribs, the stark black tattoos that mark his own becoming. She wants to place a kiss on each moth, to trace the unicorn on his back with her tongue. But she can only stand here, waiting. Because that's what he wants her to do. Because this is her gift to him.

She will give him what he wants, and gladly, because he has given her everything, everything, everything she's ever wanted.

A song starts up somewhere—

No, *the* song.

The one they sang today.

It has been mastered, perfected, with a longer intro than they played.

Jesper's hands wrap around her upper arms, and he pushes her back, step by step, gentle but implacable. She trusts him; he won't let her fall. Only when she stumbles over a familiar lump does she recall the Turkish rugs on the floor last night— this morning? Yesterday? When was it? What is time?

As he lifts her left arm, she realizes what is happening.

The X. The St. Andrew's Cross. He is going to put her wrists in the softly lined manacles.

He is going to tie her up, just like he said.

Something different.

Something he's been fantasizing about.

The cuff is already around her wrist. He buckles it tightly— More so than last time.

"It's a little tight," she says playfully, hoping it doesn't sound like a complaint.

"It's meant to be, little angel." He sucks on her earlobe, kisses down her neck to the hollow of her throat, leaves her shivering. "That's what makes it so hot."

He takes her other wrist, and—

She can't—

She doesn't want—

Full animal panic sets in.

The last time she was cuffed to this thing, there were other people, cameras, it was planned. She panicked, but ultimately, she was safe. And she wants to feel safe with Jesper — she *does* feel safe with him — but she doesn't want to be completely tied down, unable to move. She doesn't trust anyone that much. Just the thought of it makes her want to throw her head and scream like a horse.

She rips her right arm out of his grasp and tears off the blindfold.

She'd expected to see Jesper standing there naked, but...

The entire band is here.

And so is the man in the unicorn mask.

Unicorn, rabbit, stag, and owl
Unleash your beast, prepare to howl
You're only free behind the mask
Want to kill? To die? Just ask
We light our candles, carve the rune
Whet the knife and call the moon

"THESE ARE NOT MY REAL EYES," TRACK #4 ON BLACK IDYLL,
THE SUCCULENT REAPING, KAKOPHONY RECORDS, 2024.

23

Angelina's muddled brain snaps back into place.

She's drunk, but she is suddenly not *that* drunk.

Not so drunk that any of this is reasonable.

The room looks almost exactly as it did when they recorded the video. Iron candle stands covered in red and black candles. Walls draped in blood-red velvet. Ah, but one of the rugs has been removed, revealing a black stone floor with a circle painted in white, the pentacle within covered in strange letters that seem to squirm like maggots. The soft thing she sat on while Jesper removed her shoes is a wooden altar, old and carved with runes, a white sheepskin thoughtfully draped over one edge. Her eye is drawn to a large knife sitting in the center of it, a cruel thing with a shining silver blade and a hilt of twisted black horn.

The other bandmates wear nothing but their robes and masks—stag, rabbit, owl. One holds a bowl, one holds a goblet, and one holds a—

Jesus Christ. A stack of papers.

Are they—

Is this—

There are no cameras.

Whatever this is, it's real, or they think it is.

"Angelina—" Jesper starts.

He's the only one not wearing his mask, and the look on his face—

He is shocked.

And terrified.

Absolutely terrified.

"No!" she shouts. "No!"

But he moves toward her, reaching for her wrist.

She can't let him have it, can't let him touch her again.

The thought is sickening.

He—

He was using her.

For something.

Whatever this is.

She screams as she kicks him, aiming for his quickly dying erection. When her foot connects, he stumbles backward, grabbing for himself, growling like an animal. He falls into one of the robed band members, and in the chaos, Angelina reaches for her cuffed wrist and plucks at the leather. She gets the end untucked but can't quite—

She's not fast enough.

Solomon is on her now, in his stupid owl mask, reaching for her free hand. She knows she's not stronger than him, and he's got her fingers in his pitiless grasp, tugging her wrist toward the other cuff. Ah, but he's so much taller than she is, and he's still in his mask, and he's entirely focused on her hand. She bends her head to his pierced nipple, grasps the bar in her teeth, and viciously yanks it free.

He whirls away in a spurt of blood, clutching at the hole where his nipple once was, and she spits it out onto the ground, her mouth full of the cold tang of copper and the astringent flavor of his favorite cedar cologne. She nearly gags, but she doesn't have time for that shit. She has to get out of here.

She again goes for the cuff, but now it's Nico facing off with her. Big, strong Nico who puts bad guys in choke holds and doles out black eyes to paparazzi. He rips off the stag mask, and his beautiful, sunny face is suffused with rage and panic.

"Not tonight, little girl," he barks.

He rears back to punch her—

Nico!

Drummer of Black Idyll!

Is naked!

And punching her—

She dodges at the last minute. His fist bashes into the heavy wood of the cross, and he sucks in a breath and cradles his knuckles. It's the same hand he used to hit the paparazzo earlier. In the split second that he's hissing over his busted flesh, Angelina reaches up and works the buckle free on the manacle. Her hand is asleep, but oh God, freedom is so sweet! She looks to the door, and—

Nico grabs her neck with his good hand, pinching on the sides.

She tries to pull away, but he presses her back against the wood cross. The world starts to flutter around her—he's cutting off the blood—

Her legs collapse, and Nico isn't prepared to hold the dead weight in his non-dominant hand. He drops her, and she lands on the ground on her knees. They hurt like hell, but the rug helped soften the blow. She'll feel the pain later, if she lives through this—

This—

Whatever this is.

She's crawling for the door when Nico grabs her around the waist, but as he pulls her to standing, she grabs for the nearest weapon—

Well, it wasn't a weapon, but it is now.

It's the leopard-shaped brass candle snuffer, and she wraps her fingers around it and twists, jabbing the leopard's reaching paw into Nico's eye.

He drops her and falls back, scrabbling at his face as blood pours down.

"What did you do, you bitch?" he roars, and somewhere in Angelina's shattered psyche she wishes she could show a recording of this moment to the charity that honored Nico with an award for his commitment to raising awareness of violence against women.

She knows she only has seconds before one of them grabs her, and she knows she'll have trouble surprising any of them again, not after what she just did to Nico. Fingers wrap around her ankle, and she yanks as hard as she can, throwing herself onto the altar table and grabbing the knife while it's under her body. The ridges of the twisted horn hilt hurt her fingers as she finds the sturdiest handhold.

"Angelina, you consented," Jesper growls, his beautiful voice fierce and cruel. "You agreed to this, over and over. You gave your word."

He claws himself up her body, his fingers pinching up her calf, her thigh, her waist, until he's got her by the shoulders, prying her up from the table. She gathers one hand underneath her, knowing she only has one last push before they all converge.

"This isn't personal," he whispers. "I really do love you. That's how it works."

He nearly yanks her left arm out of the socket pulling her back to standing.

As he spins her around, she slams the knife into his side.

Welcome to the worst day of your life
It's time to face the bloodied butcher's knife
The razor's edge between then and now
Are you the abattoir or the suckling cow?

"FACE THE KNIFE," TRACK #2 ON BLACK IDYLL,
(RE)HEARSE, KAKOPHONY RECORDS, 2014.

24

For a moment, Jesper Idyll stands there, stark and white and beautiful as a marble statue of a demigod. But Angelina no longer trusts anything, and she's watched a lot of horror movies, so she holds on to the knife and drags it upward until it slams into a rib.

"You stabbed me," he says with the wondering innocence of a child.

He falls to his knees before her.

"Welcome to the worst day of your life," she croons. "It's time to face the bloodied butcher's knife, you asshole."

She watches his mouth work as he melts to lay curled on his side; he's like a toy running out of batteries. Everything is strangely crystal clear, her body on high alert. She senses someone moving, and she squats to tear the knife out of Jesper's side and holds it out toward Solomon.

"Don't," she warns him. "Fucking don't."

For a long moment, they regard each other as Nico

writhes on the floor. And then Solomon straightens and lets out a fluttering laugh, one hand cupped over the hole in his chest. "So you've chosen the abattoir. That's what I get for offering you a choice." He waves her off like he's done with her and sits down on the sheepskin, naked as the morning. Looking down at his pectoral, he hisses in annoyance.

She next looks to Manny. He stands like a statue, dumbly holding the pile of papers—a contract, neatly held by a binder clip. "Are you going to fight me?" she asks him. He mutely shakes his head.

And then Angelina looks to the man in the unicorn mask, who sits in a black wood throne carved with moons and runes and stars. He is exactly as she remembers from the church and the storm, but now she can fully appreciate how wrong he is, how alien. With a wet, creaking noise, he stands, unfolding, too tall, disjointed, cadaverously thin, and holds something out to her on the palm of his claw-tipped hand. The unicorn mask is not a mask.

It's his head.

A man with a unicorn's head.

No.

Not a man.

Definitely not a man.

"What the fuck is that?" she asks the room at large.

The figure doesn't move, doesn't speak.

Manny offers her the contract with shaking hands.

She reads it.

The whole thing.

She knows his name now, the unicorn man.

The demon.

Amdusias, a duke of hell.

While Nico cries with his remaining eye and Solomon sits with a hand clutching his chest and Manny stands trembling in a puddle of piss and Jesper Idyll bleeds out on a Turkish rug, Angelina reads the contract from front to back.

She takes the black quill the demon offers her, dips it in the ragged, bloody hole in Jesper's side, scratches out his name on the contract, and signs her own name on the line.

Welcome to the best day of your life
It's time to face the bloodied black horn knife
The razor's edge between then and now
Are you the abattoir or the suckling cow?
I choose life, I choose death
I choose to steal your sucking breath
With your blood I'll sign my name
Give me beauty, give me fame

"KNIFE THE FACE," TRACK #1 ON WHITE IDYLL,
(RE)BIRTH, KAKOPHONY RECORDS, 2025.

AFTER

INTERVIEWER:

SO HOW IS THE BAND GETTING ALONG WITHOUT JESPER? MANY WOULD SAY HE WAS THE HEART OF BLACK IDYLL.

ANGELINE IDYLL:

DID YOU KNOW THEY CAN DO HEART TRANSPLANTS NOW? YOU CAN PUT A STETHOSCOPE TO MY CHEST AND HEAR JESPER, IF YOU WANT TO. THE BAND WILL CONTINUE ON. WHITE IDYLL IS HERE TO STAY. WE'RE A FAMILY. A COMMUNITY. AND HOUSE OF IDYLL WILL CONTINUE TO NURTURE ARTISTS AND MUSICIANS FROM ALL OVER THE WORLD IN OUR ONGOING COMMITMENT TO SPREADING BEAUTY AND PASSION WITH OUR GOOD FORTUNE.

INTERVIEWER:

YOU AND JESPER WERE DATING. DO YOU MISS HIM?

ANGELINE IDYLL:

EVERY DAY. WE WERE TWO BEASTS CALLING ACROSS A STARLIT VALLEY, AND NOW THERE IS NO ANSWER TO MY CALL. I'VE NEVER LET SOMEONE CRAWL INSIDE OF ME LIKE THAT. AND I'M FAIRLY CERTAIN I'M THE FIRST PERSON JESPER ALLOWED TO SEE HIS TRUE SELF, HIS DEEPEST SELF. I'VE SEEN INSIDE HIM, AND WHAT I SAW WAS BEAUTIFUL AND RARE AND SPECIAL, AND I WILL CARRY IT WITH ME ALWAYS.

INTERVIEWER:

THE TENTH ANNIVERSARY TOUR IS SOLD OUT. EVERYONE IS EMBRACING THE NAME CHANGE AND YOUR FANS ARE ALL WEARING WHITE. YOUR LATEST ALBUM—*YOUR* FIRST ALBUM, THAT IS, AND THE BAND'S LATEST ALBUM—WENT PLATINUM AND HIT NUMBER ONE ON THE CHARTS. WHAT DO YOU HAVE TO SAY TO YOUR FANS?

ANGELINE IDYLL:

IN JESPER'S WORDS, ONLY COWARDS RUN. THE EDGE OF THE CLIFF IS THE STARTING GUN. AND I HIGHLY ADVISE STEPPING OFF THE CLIFF AND SEEING WHERE IT TAKES YOU.

~~THE END~~
THE BEGINNING

ABOUT THE AUTHOR

DELILAH S. DAWSON is the *New York Times*-bestselling and Bram Stoker Award®-nominated author of *Guillotine*, *Bloom*, *The Violence*, *It Will Only Hurt For A Moment*, *Ride or Die*, *Mine*, *Camp Scare*, the Blud series, the Hit series, *Servants of the Storm*, *Midnight at the Houdini*, several *Star Wars* books, and the Shadow series, written as Lila Bowen. She once saw The Living Unicorn at the circus as a child and has never recovered.

Find her online at www.delilahsdawson.com and on social media, @delilahsdawson.

BLOOM

Delilah S. Dawson

Rosemary meets Ash at the farmers' market. Ash—precise, pretty, and practically perfect—sells bars of soap in delicate pastel colors, sprinkle-spackled cupcakes stacked on scalloped stands, beeswax candles, jelly jars of honey, and glossy green plants.

Ro has never felt this way about another woman; with Ash, she wants to be her and have her in equal measure. But as her obsession with Ash consumes her, she may find she's not the one doing the devouring…

Told in lush, delectable prose, this is a deliciously dark tale of passion taking an unsavory turn…

—◇—

"A slim novel with incredible potency. A literary pursuit for the ages. I can't recall a courtship as captivating as the one in these pages, and if there's a better writer than Delilah Dawson going today, I don't know 'em."

JOSH MALERMAN, *New York Times* bestselling author of *Bird Box* and *Incidents Around the House*

"A cottagecore dream turned nightmare, astonishing in its beauty and violence. Every page drips with delicious dread. This bite-sized tale is perfectly wicked."

RACHEL HARRISON, *USA Today* bestselling author of *So Thirsty* and *Play Nice*

TITANBOOKS.COM

GUILLOTINE

Delilah S. Dawson

Thrift fashionista Dez Lane doesn't want to date Patrick Ruskin; she just wants to meet his mother, the editor-in-chief of *Nouveau* magazine. When he invites her to his family's big Easter reunion at their ancestral home, she's certain she can put up with his arrogance and fend off his advances long enough to ask Marie Caulfield-Ruskin for an internship someone with her pedigree could never nab through the regular submission route.

When they arrive at the enormous island mansion, Dez is floored — she's never witnessed how the 1% lives before in all their ridiculous, unnecessary luxury. But once all the family members are on the island and the ferry has departed, things take a dark turn. For decades, the Ruskins have made their servants sign contracts that are basically indentured servitude, and with nothing to lose, the servants have decided their only route to freedom is to get rid of the Ruskins for good…

The Menu meets *Ready or Not* in this dark tale of opulent luxury and shocking violence from the *New York Times* bestselling author of *Bloom*.

—◇—

"Fast, fun, and frightening, *Glass Onion* meets
Saw in this savagely on-point thriller."

T. KINGFISHER, the *New York Times* bestselling author
of *What Moves the Dead* and *The Twisted Ones*

"Deliciously brutal and stiletto sharp. *Guillotine* is the
eat-the-rich horror you've been waiting for."

RORY POWER, the *New York Times* bestselling author
of *Wilder Girls* and *In a Garden Burning Gold*

For more fantastic fiction, author events,
exclusive excerpts, competitions, limited editions and more

VISIT OUR WEBSITE
titanbooks.com

LIKE US ON FACEBOOK
facebook.com/titanbooks

FOLLOW US ON TWITTER AND INSTAGRAM
@TitanBooks

EMAIL US
readerfeedback@titanemail.com

Chic to Geek

or little girl, all alone in the dark
le doesn't know her bite is worse than hi
e thinks it's pity, he thinks she's pretty
Soon his neck will wear her mark
Chic to geek, cool to freak
High school's pretty fucking bleak, oh yeah

3. Pretty Boys Don't Cry

Have you ever felt so alone that you wa
Have you ever felt so alone that you
(But pretty boys don't cry)
Have you ever felt like just a tiny pi
(See the comets passing by)
So far away from the Earth you kr
Yet you're stuck on cursed groun

4. Trust the Snake

In the garden of Eden, no crime
The line between innocence and
We ended up naked but started ou
Eve didn't feign hunger when Ad
Ignorance, a barbed-wire fence
Set me up for failure and shit'

(Re)Hearse
 akophony Records, 2014

Un1c0rn

can't run and you can't hide
d you almost live or have you almost died
ey told you to blend in with the herd
But conformity is a dirty word
You're a unicorn, you're a unicorn
From your blade-edged hooves to your stabb
Be tall and proud
Get big, get loud
Be their number one, not tragedy porn

2. Face the Knife

Welcome to the worst day of your life
It's time to face the bloodied butcher's kr
The razor's edge between then and now
Are you the abattoir or the suckling cow?

3. Kiss Kiss KMS

Sometimes it's just too much
A child can die from lack of touch
And me, I'm just a child
Trapped in this skeleton, tender and mi
Release would be so sweet
om pain to meat

ng That Kills (Unreleased

Maybe a ghost is what we need.
The living aren't giving, they're full of g
When you've already lost, when you're
A queen can never be a pawn.
Fall in love, fall to your knees
Her hive is filled with adoring bees
Each sting kills not one but two
Each sting kills both me and you

From the personal collection of Jesper Idyll.

The Succulent Reaping
Kakophony Records, 2024

1. Sleep No More

In the darkest part of the darkest night
He wakes and walks in the fire's light
Why do you keep hidden, I want to ask
Why do you wear that human mask?

3. Love Song of the Moth

The nights are long, but life is short
This death is not a petite mort
Live big, live fast, die young, it's past
Your days are numbered, time is vast
To brightly shine take my advice
Crave the glory, pay the price

4. These Are Not My Real Eyes

Unicorn, rabbit, stag, and owl
Unleash your beast, prepare to howl
You're only free behind the mask
Want to kill? To die? Just ask
light our candles, carve the rune
et the knife and call the moon

ong of Becoming
life I've